**"Are you always going to be
this chatty when I try
to make love to you?"
Moss asked with mild interest.**

Alarmed at the immediate response singing through her body at his touch, Kat strove for matching flippancy. "I don't know. Are you going to try to make love to me often?"

"Oh, yes," he promised with a seductive smile. "Very, very often. Starting now." As Kat gasped in surprise and pleasure, he rolled deftly on top of her, his considerable weight pinning her down into the forgiving softness of the beanbag chair.

"I feel it only fair to warn you," she said with a last-ditch effort at self-control, "that I'm not very good at this."

"I'll take my chances." Moss nuzzled her throat.

"Moss," she whispered, "Moss, we shouldn't—"

"Probably not," he agreed, his voice as low as hers, "but when the hell have either of us done what we should?"

Laine Allen is a happily married mother of two. In addition to her family, she loves "good food, good wine, romantic movies, and just about any kind of music." A voracious reader and "fairly good" tennis player, she has traveled extensively through Europe, living briefly in Holland and Germany. Originally from California, she now resides on an acre and a half of evergreen woods in Upstate New York.

Dear Reader:

The lazy days of summer are here, a perfect time to enjoy July's SECOND CHANCE AT LOVE romances.

In *Master Touch* (#274) Jasmine Craig reintroduces Hollywood idol Damion Tanner, who you'll remember as Lynn Frampton's boss in *Dear Adam* (#243). Damion *looks* like a typical devastating womanizer, but inside he's a man of intriguing depth, complexity, and contradictory impulses. He dislikes Alessandra Hawkins on sight, but can't resist pursuing her. Alessandra is thoroughly disdainful of Damion, and equally smitten. You'll love reading how these two marvelously antagonistic characters walk backward into love — resisting all the way!

In *Night of a Thousand Stars* (#275) Petra Diamond takes you where no couple has gone before — to sex in space! Astronaut Jennie Jacobs and ace pilot Dean Bradshaw have *all* the "right stuff" for such an experiment, but they've had little time to explore their more tender feelings. Suddenly their emotions catch up with them, making their coming together a bristly, challenging proposition. Petra Diamond handles their love story with sensitive realism, making *Night of a Thousand Stars* out of this world.

Laine Allen, an exciting newcomer, turns romance stereotypes on their heads in *Undercover Kisses* (#276). Every time private eye Katrina Langley asks herself, "How wrong could a woman be about a man," ultra-manly Moss Adams suggests the answer: "Very wrong!" Every time Kat thinks they're evenly matched, Moss cheerfully knocks her off balance. Moss's intelligent deviltry and Kat's swift-witted ripostes will keep you chuckling as you discover the secrets they keep from each other, while unraveling a most perplexing intrigue.

SECOND CHANCE AT LOVE is pleased to introduce another new writer — Elizabeth Henry, author of *Man Trouble* (#277). Like other heroines you've met, Marcy has a low opinion of men — especially Rick Davenport, who climbs through her bedroom window after midnight and challenges her to all sorts of fun and games. But no other heroine must contend with an alter ego called Nosy, who butts in with unasked-for advice. Nonstop banter makes *Man Trouble* as light, crunchy, and fun to consume as popcorn.

In *Suddenly That Summer* (#278) by Jennifer Rose, Carrie Delaney's so fed up with the dating game that she spends a week at a tacky singles resort, determined to find a husband. But she's so busy participating in the toga party, forest scavenger hunt, and after-dark skinny dip that she refuses to recognize the man of her dreams — even when he insists he's "it"! Thank goodness James Luddington has the cleverness and persistence to win Carrie by fair means or foul. Finding a mate has never been so confusing — or so much fun!

In *Sweet Enchantment* (#279), Diana Mars employs warmth and skill to convey the joys and heartaches of combining two families into one through a new marriage. Pamela Shaw, whom you know as Barrett Shaw's sister-in-law in *Sweet Trespass* (#182), has to deal with her son's antagonism toward her new love, Grady Talliver, *and* with Grady's four young sons. But lizards in the bathroom, a bed sprayed with perfume, and a chamber of horrors in the attic don't ruffle our heroine, who more than adequately turns the tables on her little darlings. *Sweet Enchantment* is a story many of you will identify with — and all of you will enjoy.

Have fun!

Ellen Edwards

Ellen Edwards, Senior Editor
SECOND CHANCE AT LOVE
The Berkley Publishing Group
200 Madison Avenue
New York, N.Y. 10016

Second Chance at Love

UNDERCOVER KISSES

LAINE ALLEN

A
SECOND CHANCE AT LOVE
BOOK

UNDERCOVER KISSES

First edition published July 1985

First printing

"Second Chance at Love" and the butterfly emblem are trademarks belonging to Jove Publications, Inc.

Printed in the United States of America

Second Chance at Love books are published by
The Berkley Publishing Group
200 Madison Avenue, New York, NY 10016

To Alan,

who is everything a hero ought to be
—and more

CHAPTER
One

IN THE DISTANCE the glittering waters of San Francisco Bay sparkled as though the surface had been scattered with silver leaves, but Kat barely noticed either the spectacular view of Alcatraz or the cable car rumbling past with its tightly clinging human cargo. Her mind was riveted on her upcoming interview.

Slowing down for yet another stoplight, she glanced at the Miss Piggy watch peeking out from under her sleeve and could have screamed. She had exactly fourteen minutes to find the photography studio, locate a parking place, and then figure out how she was going to wriggle out of her ravaged panty hose in the middle of a public thoroughfare before she had to face Mark Adams. She'd never make it.

Of all the times to run her nylons! Today she had wanted to look elegantly professional. Specifically, she'd wanted to look like the most dazzlingly efficient secretary Mark Adams had ever laid eyes on.

No one, Kat conceded ruefully, could possibly be less qualified for the role. Oh, she was capable of doing the job, but dazzling efficiency implied something almost superhuman: It implied being on time. As manager and sole employee of her own fledgling investigative agency, Kat had a lot of valuable qualities to offer a prospective employer. Punctuality, unfortunately, just wasn't one of them. Which was why she'd wanted to look neat, tidy, and full of potential. How on earth was she going to manage it looking like something the cat dragged in?

Kat glared at the traffic light, willing it to turn green. It did, but the bumper-to-bumper cars clogging the street barely crawled. Tucking a wayward strand of auburn hair into the comb behind her ear, she peered impatiently over the low black Corvette ahead of her to see what the problem was. A cluster of buildings snagged her attention. Was that a department store ahead? It was! Kat did a quick mental calculation. If she was very, very quick, she had just enough time to buy a new pair of hose, change into them, and still make it to her destination—only two blocks now—reasonably on time. It would have to be the quickest purchase of her life, but she could manage it—just—if she was—

Kat flicked a glance back down at the Corvette and let out a horrified "Oh, no!" It had stopped. Even as her foot moved toward the brake she knew it was too late. Hands clutching the steering wheel, she braced herself for the inevitable impact. It came less than two seconds later, accompanied by the sickening sound of metal grinding against metal and the tinkle of shattering glass.

For a moment Kate just sat there, too stunned to move. Then, very slowly, she opened her eyes. The hood of her car looked shorter, the black car was definitely too close for comfort, but at least she was still in one piece. A dull ache was already making itself known across her shoulders, but what concerned her most was that there was no discernible movement in the car ahead. Was the other driver hurt? A finger of icy fear traveled down her spine. Why in heaven's name hadn't she watched the road?

Fumbling with her seat belt, Kat threw open the door of her battered Toyota and hopped out. Ignoring the honking car swerving dangerously close to her, she rushed forward to the Corvette. She wasn't quite even with the driver's door when the window rolled down. Relieved, because at least the movement indicated the occupant wasn't unconscious, Kat leaned over.

"Excuse me, are you all—"

A deep male voice cut her off. "Get back in your car before you get run over," it growled with crisp authority.

Kat knew the advice was sensible, but she wasn't at all sure she liked the way it had been delivered. Glimpsing a pair of strong, darkly tanned hands resting on the leather-wrapped steering wheel, it occurred to her that their owner couldn't be in *too* much pain if he had the strength to snap out orders.

Trying to put a face with those hands, Kat bent down farther. "I just came up to see if you were hurt. If you're not—"

This time more than just her words were cut off as a bronzed hand snaked out the window and grabbed the belt of her dress, pulling her so close to the shiny Corvette she could barely breathe. The protest forming on her lips died as a Cadillac, horn blaring, charged past her with less than an inch of room to spare.

"I'm not," the man in the black car told her, calmly releasing her belt again, "but if you insist on standing in traffic, I'm not sure how long we'll be able to say that about you. There's a shopping mall just ahead. Pull into the parking lot, and we can talk all you want." Shifting the sports car into gear, he eased it forward.

Kat stared at the moving vehicle in frustration. "I don't have time to talk!" she wailed.

By the time Kat pulled into the parking lot behind the sleek black car, four more precious minutes out of her original fourteen were gone. Jumping out of her Toyota, she marched briskly across the pavement. She would be firm. She would be polite. And then she would be on her way. Otherwise, she was going to be hopelessly late.

"Look," she said, approaching the other car, "I'd love to stay and chat with you, but—"

Kat's words stopped in her throat as the blond man seated behind the steering wheel eased his lean, long-limbed frame out of the low-slung sports car.

Kat swallowed. He was, without any doubt, the tallest, tannest, toughest-looking man she'd ever met, and every muscled inch of him radiated thoroughly masculine annoyance.

"Don't stop now," he urged smoothly, standing so close to Kat that she caught a whiff of his woodsy after shave. "Things were just beginning to get interesting. You were saying?"

Even though she was an Amazonian five feet ten in heels, Kat had to tilt her chin up just to look at him. What *had* she been saying? She'd forgotten. Lord, he was a big brute! A good-looking one, too—or would have been if his firm, no-nonsense mouth had been just a shade fuller. Dressed in snug jeans and a blue shirt with the sleeves rolled up on his sinewy forearms, he looked rough and athletic, capable of leaping tall buildings in a single bound. Definitely not the sort of man you wanted to tangle with in a dark alley. Or in the middle of a busy intersection, for that matter.

Resisting the urge to hop back into her car, Kat surreptitiously wiped her damp palms on the skirt of her wool dress. Did he have any idea how nervous he was making her? Yes, of course he did. He'd have to be a fool not to, and somehow he didn't look like a fool.

She cleared her throat. "Yes, well...I...ah...mmm..."

As she stuttered, he removed his wire-rimmed aviator sunglasses. Kat's heart started to thump against her ribs. Before now she had always thought of gray eyes as pale and cold, but his were dark and smoking hot. And, at the moment, they were undressing her garment by garment, working their way down to her black bikini panties with alarming rapidity.

It was the impetus her brain needed to start functioning again. Drawing herself up to her full height, which still fell woefully short of his, Kat put her hands on her hips and gave him a long, less encouraging stare of her own.

"What do you think you're doing?"

The molten-gray eyes rose slowly to meet hers. "Looking

at you," he admitted, sounding perfectly at ease. "That was quite a smash-up back there. I take it you're not hurt?"

He obviously wasn't. It would probably take an armored tank division to do him damage, and even then she wouldn't have bet on it.

Kat gave him a disparaging look. "I'm not made of glass."

His golden eyebrows, two shades darker than his gilded hair, rose in surprise. "My, my," he said mildly, "I guess we can eliminate sugar and spice, too. You're a very aggressive woman, aren't you?"

Kat's smile could easily have caused cavities. "Sorry to disappoint you."

"Do I look disappointed?"

No, actually he looked as if he'd just been handed a delightful present. What he didn't seem to realize was that she had no intention of being unwrapped.

Estimating he'd just handily divested her of her lacy scrap of a bra, Kat pointedly flicked a quick look at her watch. "I don't want to be rude, but do you suppose we could take care of this?" She motioned toward the two mangled cars. "I'm in a hurry."

"Hot date?"

Despite herself, Kat warmed at the interested query. "That's none of your business. Are you always this forward?"

"Are you always this quick on the trigger?"

"I haven't shot anyone. Yet."

Looking vaguely amused but not particularly threatened by the implied threat, he bent down beside the Corvette and assessed the destruction she'd wrought. Wetting her lips, Kat chastised herself even as she secretly admired the way his shirt stretched tautly across his smoothly muscled back. What in the world was wrong with her? At twenty-six she wasn't exactly unused to male interest. Sometimes she liked it, most of the time she didn't, but normally it didn't bother her because she knew she could take care of herself. She certainly wasn't the type of woman who palpitated when a man simply looked at her.

Of course, no man had ever looked at her quite the way this blond behemoth had.

What, she wondered, did he do for a living? That tan hadn't come from an occasional game of tennis or golf. Neither had those muscles, which she was doing her best to ignore. Was he a lawyer? An executive? Impossible. Scratch all the normal professions. She couldn't quite see him spending his days shuffling papers around, however lucrative the business might be. He simply didn't look like a man who could ever be contained within the confines of an office.

What then? A professional athlete? Somehow she didn't think so. He looked like a loner, not the kind of man who went in for team sports. A nonconformist. Even his hair seemed to disdain conventionality. Almost defiantly unstyled and long enough to graze his collar, it was an unusual tawny shade, as thick as any lion's mane. Kat didn't doubt for a minute that, whatever he did, he was the king of his particular jungle.

Was he on the wrong side of the law? There was something shrewd and ruthless in his angular face. Whatever he did, Kat had the strangest feeling it was something unusual, possibly even dangerous. It wasn't just the scar near his left eye that gleamed white against his deep tan; it was the way he walked, the way he talked. He looked as if he'd sampled every vice known to man . . . and then invented a few of his own.

The spiky brown eyelashes, dark in contrast to his hair, suddenly rose. Caught openly staring at him, Kat whirled away. Her gaze landed on her own car, and she let out an involuntary moan. In addition to a crushed grill, it had a broken headlight and a front bumper that looked as if it had tangled with a garbage disposal and lost.

"If you think that's upsetting, wait until you see what you've done to mine."

Turning slowly, Kat found herself under the scrutiny of those hot gray eyes again. Feeling warm and prickly, she walked reluctantly around his car to where he sat on his heels. Halfway there she stopped. "I didn't do all that!" she protested.

"No," he agreed, "you had some help from a brunette in a Datsun Z on Monday. Do you see a tow bar here?" He indicated the crumpled rear bumper. When Kat mutely shook her head, his mobile mouth twisted in grim satisfaction. "No, neither do I."

Even though she was willing to admit that mild annoyance on his part was understandable, Kat was irritated at his implication that she'd been following too closely, thus causing the accident.

"I wouldn't have hit you if you hadn't slammed on your brakes," she huffed.

"Would you have preferred I run over the little old lady who was crossing the street?" he asked mildly.

Kat bit her lower lip. She hadn't seen any lady, old or otherwise. "Well, no. Of course not."

"You don't sound too sure of that."

Kat's ears warmed. "There's no need to get sarcastic. I realize I'm the one at fault—"

"Good." He rose, dusting off his large hands. "That's one less thing for us to argue about. You know, you could try showing a little remorse."

How he could make her feel guilty in ten words or less was beyond Kat, but she was feeling very guilty—although not particularly repentant. "I'm sorry about your car," she said tersely.

"Are you?"

"Yes!"

"You sound it."

"What do you want me to do, get down on my knees and grovel?"

He looked at her as though considering the suggestion. Just as she was beginning to regret the rhetorical question, he said, "No, but you could try sounding more convincing."

Kat took a deep breath. "I am very, very, very sorry I hit your car. How's that?"

"Better." He nodded in approval. "But actions speak

louder than words. Make a believer out of me. Have dinner with me tonight."

Kat simply blinked at him in disbelief. Was *that* what he'd been leading up to all this time? Maybe if she'd had more time and wasn't still so steamed at Derek . . . No. Kat immediately banished the thought. Never mind that he was dangerously attractive and had a voice sexy enough to curl a woman's toes, the last thing she needed was another man in her life.

"I guess that long silence means no."

Yanked back to the present by the amused comment, Kat found herself the subject of interested appraisal. "If you're trying to make a pass at me," she said frankly, visions of a smiling, treacherous Derek firmly implanted in her mind, "you can forget it. I'm not interested."

His smile was crooked and strangely appealing. "If there's any doubt about whether or not it was a pass, maybe I'd *better* forget it. My technique must need a brushup."

Enjoying herself more than she thought she should be, Kat smiled back at him. "Would you settle for a brush-off?" she cooed.

The gold eyebrows rose. "At this point I'd say that gun of yours was smoking, wouldn't you? What do you say we call a truce? I'm beginning to feel like one of the walking wounded."

His white teeth flashed, and she got a glimpse of the man behind the tough facade. But the smile disappeared as fast as it had come.

"What's the matter?" he barked.

The sharpness in his voice startled her. Kat stopped rubbing the back of her neck and dropped her hand almost guiltily. "Nothing. I guess I got jarred a little when I hit your—"

"Is it your neck?"

Kat assumed from the suspicious way he said it that he thought she was considering suing him. "Don't worry, I'm not going to take you to court claiming whiplash."

"Temper, temper, shortstuff. Goodness, you're a suspicious woman. Feisty, too. But that's okay; I like to see a woman stand up for herself."

Before Kat knew what he was going to do, he'd placed his long-fingered hands on her shoulders and firmly turned her around.

"Tell me when it hurts," he ordered, gently pressing his thumbs against the tendons at the base of her neck and then sliding them slowly down her spine.

"Will you please remove your hands from my—ouch!" Kat gasped in outrage and pain.

"That's tender, is it? How about here?" His strong fingers moved up across her shoulder blades in careful exploration.

"Are you a doctor?" Kat demanded.

"Nope."

"Then will you kindly take your hands off—" Her teeth snapped together before she could finish.

"That hurts, too, does it? Must have been your seat belt. Good thing you were wearing it or you might have been hurt a lot worse. You're going to have some bruises to-morrow."

"So are you," said Kat through her teeth, "if you don't take your hands off me."

His laugh was warm and sexy, and it sent an unexpected wave of silver heat coursing through her veins. "Relax." His warm hands slid up to her neck. "I'm trying to figure out if anything's fractured."

Kat closed her eyes, fighting the onslaught of sensations his touch was inciting. "Have you ever tried to relax with someone's hands around your throat?"

"Worried?" There was a distinct smile in his voice. "Don't be. I'm not usually prone to violence. Though for a minute there I could have cheerfully strangled you for what you did to my car. Of course, that was before I noticed what a lovely neck you have."

The next thing Kat knew, his fingers were stroking the sensitive spot behind her right ear, igniting a flare of desire deep within her. Her eyes flew open in alarm.

"Stop that!" she breathed, spinning around to face him.

"Sorry." He looked impossibly contrite. "Just checking for sprains. How's your neck? Better?"

Afraid if she said no he'd latch on to her again, Kat said quickly, "It's fine. Thank you. I think."

His smoky gray eyes focused on her mouth. "Any time."

Lord, he sounded serious! Things were definitely getting out of hand. *He* certainly was.

"Yes, well, about your car—" Kat began briskly.

He shrugged. "Don't worry about it. I'm sure your insurance will cover the damage. Who's your insurance agent?"

Kat had been hoping he wouldn't ask. "Well . . ."

He lifted a large hand to silence her. "Don't tell me, let me guess. You don't have insurance."

"Of course I have insurance," Kat retorted. "But I can't afford to have my premiums go up any higher than they are already. Just because I'm a woman doesn't mean I'm a fool."

He shook his head. "I seem to have pushed the wrong button again. You're determined to take offense, aren't you?"

"You've been giving me lots of encouragement!"

"Wish I could say the same for you."

Kat ignored the complaint. "I suppose I could pay for the repairs myself," she offered tentatively, though with what she didn't know. Her investigative agency wasn't exactly hauling in profits at this point.

The sexy blond stranger looked from her seen-better-days Toyota back to her with heart-stopping interest. "That sounds promising. What kind of compensation did you have in mind?"

Kat took a deep breath. That was it. Those suggestive words were the last straw. She'd tried to be reasonable, but reason was obviously the last thing he wanted from her. "Are you quite through propositioning me?" she asked with all the ardor-dampening calm she could muster. "You are? Good."

Giving him no chance to answer whether he was finished or not, Kat took a pen and a scrap of paper from her purse and scribbled down her name, address, and phone number. Reaching up, she shoved it into his shirt pocket and tried to ignore the warm, firmly muscled body beneath the soft blue fabric.

"When you get the bill for repairs," she told him, "send

it to me at this address. And if by then I've managed to forget that last comment I may, just may, decide to reimburse you. Now if you'll excuse me." Smiling brightly, she climbed back into her Toyota and started it with a satisfying roar. "I have a very important appointment, and you've already made me late."

But even as she drove off, Kat knew it wasn't him she was really irritated with. It was Derek. It was always Derek.

CHAPTER
Two

CAREFUL NOT TO damage her newly purchased hosiery, Kat closed and locked the door of her battered Toyota and thoughtfully studied the tasteful adobe building that housed Mark Adams's photography studio. She honestly didn't know what she'd expected, but this totally captivating, compactly designed, red-tile-roofed building, with its Moorish arches and courtyard entry garden, certainly wasn't it.

What had Ken said that day when he'd unintentionally spurred her thinking process into high gear? That strange things were happening at Mark Adams's studio. That numerous instances of sabotage were scaring off not only Adams's models but his office help as well. Adams had reportedly hired half a dozen different secretaries in the past two months, and only one had stayed more than two weeks.

Seeing his sister's sudden rapt interest and correctly interpreting it, Ken had then tried to discourage Kat, muttering, "You'd have to be pretty desperate to even consider this one." Which, of course, had described Kat perfectly.

She was a private investigator in need of a good case. And if that case wouldn't come to her, then she'd go to it.

Someone was apparently trying to put Mark Adams out of business. Why shouldn't she be the one to figure out who and why and, she hoped, establish her reputation as a competent investigator? Sabotage might not be the crime of the century, but beggars couldn't be choosers. All Kat wanted was a foot in the door. No one was going to take her seriously until she proved she could do more than track down recalcitrant fathers overdue on their child-support payments. And if that meant getting herself hired somewhat underhandedly as a secretary so she could tackle the job from the "inside" ... well, so be it. It was, she was sure, the only way Mark Adams was going to welcome her.

Slinging the strap of her purse over her shoulder, Kat surveyed the building once again as she strode purposefully across the parking lot. Sabotage aside, there was always the possibility that no one wanted to work for Mark Adams because he was an ogre. At the moment, Kat didn't care if he was Genghis Khan reincarnated; she was going to march in there and convince the man she was indispensable.

A soft, bell-like ping announced her arrival. As her brown suede heels sank into lavishly thick green carpet, Kat took in the office. Airy and spacious, flooded with sun from a skylight, the blue-and-green room gave an impression of quiet serenity. But the harried-looking man with the Nikon strung around his neck looked anything but composed.

Choking off a muttered obscenity as the door behind Kat whispered shut, he glanced up, his hazel eyes flicking over her with obviously frayed patience. "Your bone structure is terrific, but I don't get much call for redheads. Sorry."

The rapped-out summation surprised her. Not an ogre, perhaps, but definitely not a saint either, Kat decided. Undeterred, she offered her hand. "I'm not a model. My name is Katrina Langley. I have an interview with Mr. Adams about the secretarial position.

She hadn't realized how tense she was until she heard her voice, usually quite husky, flute up at least half an octave. She almost sighed aloud in relief when the man behind the littered desk put down the eight-by-ten photo he was holding and extended a well-manicured hand.

"I'm Mark Adams," he admitted in wry apology. "Sorry
I barked. It's been an unusually frustrating day." Smoothing
back his dark brown hair, he beckoned her toward an adjoining room. "Come on into the studio. We're less likely
to be interrupted there."

Kat followed him into a large studio liberally papered
with blowups of beautiful faces and cluttered with an assortment of camera equipment and other, stranger para-
phernalia.

"Props," Mark Adams explained. "I was just about to
make myself a cup of coffee. Would you like some?"

Startled by the offer—surely a sign that the man had at
least some degree of sensitivity—Kat smiled. "I'd love some,
thank you."

Mark Adams smiled back. "Don't thank me yet. You
haven't tasted it. I'm still trying to figure out how to work
the damned machine. I hope you take yours with cream or
sugar."

"Actually, I take both."

"Good. Otherwise it's barely drinkable." He offered her
a canvas director's chair. "Make yourself comfortable. It'll
only take a second."

Kat sat down next to a pedestal table that looked like an
elephant's foot and watched as he puttered around with the
coffeepot. This was the man Ken claimed no one wanted
to work for? So far, nothing was turning out quite the way
she'd expected, including Mark Adams. The neat, vested
suit did not fit her image of what a flamboyant fashion
photographer might wear, and he was younger than she'd
thought he'd be—probably not much more than thirty. He
was also a lot friendlier than she'd expected. It would be
nice if she could just come out and *ask* him if she could
handle the investigation of his studio's problems, she thought
in regret. But past experience had taught her that just because
a man looked and sometimes acted reasonable didn't necessarily mean he was. Take Derek. Please.

"Careful." Mark Adams handed her a paper cup filled
with murky liquid. "It's hot." Parking his slim body on the
edge of the table, he smiled at her from its photo-strewn

surface. "So, you're interested in the secretarial position. Have you brought along a résumé?"

Feeling ridiculously dishonest, Kat handed over her painstakingly typed and wholly falsified *curriculum vitae* and waited for lightning to strike her where she sat. Lying about her job history was one thing, but claiming she'd once worked as an executive secretary in Derek's law firm? She just hoped Mark Adams wasn't the type who checked references! Persistent questioning of her uncooperative brother, whose art studio ran on a similar basis, had given Kat an idea of what it would take to get herself hired. So far, it seemed to be working. Mark Adams was looking suitably bedazzled.

"These are very impressive credentials," he noted, apparently accepting the manufactured information without question. "You're certainly well qualified. I don't think there'll be any problem in hiring you . . ." He paused, obviously searching for the right thing to say.

"But . . . ?" Kat prompted, her hopes dipping slightly.

"But"—Mark Adams smiled in acknowledgment—"before I do, I'd better lay all my cards on the table. I suppose you've heard we've had quite a few problems here the past few months. Yes, I can see you have. Has anyone told you why? No? Then I guess I'd better tell you. If you're seriously considering this job—and I hope you are—you're entitled to know." Pausing, he raked his fingers through his neatly combed hair. "It's because we're jinxed."

Kat wasn't sure what she'd expected him to say, but that wasn't it. "I beg your pardon?"

He lifted a hand in embarrassment. "I know it sounds ridiculous, but I don't know how else to say it. The whole damned place seems to be jinxed."

Kat didn't know quite how to respond. "Jinxed in what way?"

"In every way. In the last couple of months just about everything that can go wrong at a studio like mine has gone wrong." He ticked off a recent series of unexplained incidents on his slender fingers. "Things either disappear, fall apart, or malfunction with annoying regularity. It's gotten so bad that at least four models I know of refuse to set foot in the building. And I haven't had office help that's lasted more than two weeks in so long I never know what face to expect to see in the morning. This is where most of my interviewees get up and leave. Have I scared you off yet?" His resigned smile indicated he fully expected her to join the mass exodus.

Kat remained seated. Because she was slender and attractive, most men assumed she was helpless. But appearances could be deceiving, and in her case they were. She knew exactly how to take care of herself.

"You've called the police, of course."

Mark Adams nodded. "It was the first thing I did. But, quite frankly, with murder and mayhem being committed all over the city, their investigation of the problems here has, understandably, been placed on the back burner. It's not exactly what you might call a life-threatening situation," he noted dryly.

"If that's the case," said Kat, hoping she sounded duly concerned but not accusatory, "why have so many of your secretaries left?"

"Because they were afraid," he admitted after a moment. "You see, in addition to everything else, we've had a number of ridiculous accidents here in the office."

That information interested but didn't alarm her. Accidents happened to careless people. And despite the fact the blond man in the black Corvette probably wouldn't have believed it, she wasn't usually careless.

Kat involuntarily thought about the muscled giant she'd literally run into fifteen minutes earlier and felt her whole body go warm again. It hadn't been what he'd said that had gotten to her so much, she admitted, but how he'd said it. And even though she half suspected he'd merely been baiting her to get a reaction, that last remark had been unforgivably chauvinistic.

"Believe me," Mark Adams assured her quickly, apparently taking her thoughtful silence for consternation, "I wouldn't even consider filling the position if I thought there was any danger at all. And although there's a fair amount of responsibility involved—keeping track of which model is coming when and for what job, what props are needed, and so forth—the position pays fairly well."

He casually named a salary that nearly put Kat into catatonic shock. She coughed to hide her stunned surprise.

"That's very generous." It was ridiculously high, and they both knew it. It made Kate wonder if he was telling her the truth, the whole truth, and nothing but the truth.

"As you'll soon see, models are generally high-strung, insecure, and totally exasperating to work with. Besides that, I'm a slave driver," Mark confided with a seraphic smile. "You'll earn every penny." More seriously he added, "You know, I'm glad you're taking this all so calmly. Does this mean you'll accept the job?"

Kat tried to quell the surge of excitement racing through her. If she wanted the job, apparently it was hers. She was finally going to get a case to sink her teeth into. "When would you like me to start?"

The answer to that, Kat discovered, was "Yesterday."

After a whirlwind tour of the studio and a quick introduction to Laurel Tandy, a wafer-thin model who'd been filling in as Mark's secretary, Kat was left to figure out things on her own.

Immersed in sorting through the nest of paperwork hiding her desk and gleaning as much about the studio's workings as she could in the process, Kat had just finished memorizing the names and addresses of Mark Adams's former secretaries for future reference when he emerged from his darkroom and announced it was quitting time.

"I should have hired you six months ago," he observed, surveying her orderly desk with obvious satisfaction.

"If I'd known the salary you were paying," Kat quipped, feeling as if she'd known Mark Adams for years, not hours, "I would have applied a year ago." Gathering up the pens and stray paper clips from her desktop and dropping them into a drawer, she smiled at Mark as he approached her with a furry object dangling from his fingers.

"What on earth is that?"

"Something to start off your employment here on the

right foot." He presented the rabbit's foot to her with a flourish and grinned when she groaned at the terrible pun.

"I hope I'm not going to need this," she joked, hooking the good-luck charm on her key chain.

Slipping some photos into the corner filing cabinet, Mark said almost wistfully, "I hope you're not either."

"That comment was supposed to elicit a reassuring response," Kat informed him as she covered the typewriter. "Don't tell me you really believe the studio is jinxed?"

Mark closed the file drawer and appeared to consider the question. "Not really," he said after a moment. "But we certainly seem to be having an incredible run of bad luck lately. Why, I don't know. But I stopped being flippant about the whole thing when the electric typewriter shorted out and my last secretary got a shock that nearly curled her hair permanently." He didn't seem to notice Kat staring at the machine she'd innocently been using all afternoon. "I'm just thankful Moss is around."

Kat tore her eyes away from the typewriter. "Moss?"

"My brother," Mark explained. "Things have calmed down somewhat since he came. Ah, speak of the devil, here he is now."

Kat turned, and her automatic smile of greeting died on her lips as her gaze landed on the blond giant filling the doorway.

CHAPTER
Three

Moss Adams didn't speak at first; he simply leaned against the doorjamb and looked at her from behind his dark lenses while Kat fervently prayed for the floor to open up beneath her feet and swallow her whole.

"Hello, Moss," Mark said easily. "We were just talking about you. Meet my new secretary, Katrina Langley."

Even though the aviator sunglasses hid the upper half of Moss Adams's lean, bronzed face, Kat suspected she was probably being arrested, tried, and convicted from behind those mirrored lenses.

Of all the people in San Francisco, she inwardly wailed, why did Mark's brother have to be *him?* What was he going to do? Kat felt herself prickle in alarm. Where Mark was mild-mannered, elegantly slim, and perhaps two or three inches taller than she, Moss Adams was an aggressive sky-scraper of a man. Six feet six if he was an inch, he had to weigh well over two hundred pounds. Every ounce was sinew, muscle, and bone. Never in a million years would she have guessed the two men were brothers, and Moss, obviously recognizing that fact, was looking more amused by her stunned silence than she thought necessary.

"Hello, Katrina Langley," he purred.

Feeling like a complete imbecile, Kat smiled wanly and waited for her head to be handed to her on a platter with a few well-chosen words. Her mouth practically dropped open when, instead, Moss said to Mark, "She's a lot prettier than the last one."

"I know." Mark laughed—somewhat nervously, Kat thought—while she blushed in confusion at the unexpected compliment. "But that's not why I hired her."

One of Moss's golden eyebrows cocked. "You mean she can type?"

Mark's smile was slightly twisted as he turned to Kat. "Ignore him, Katrina," he advised, shaking his head in disapproval at his brother. "Moss is a little irritable at the moment because some idiot bashed into his car this morning." Kat's cheeks grew hot at the unintentional description of herself, but Mark missed her embarrassment as he turned his attention back to his brother. "What was it, hit and run? You didn't say when you called."

Kat winced as Moss shot her a mocking smile, but he said easily enough, "Something like that." He removed his sunglasses and hooked them on his shirt pocket. His hot gray eyes skimmed over Kat, speeding up her pulse. "I thought we decided you weren't going to fill the secretarial position for a while."

Mark suddenly looked as if his collar were too tight. "I know we agreed it might be better to wait a bit, Moss," he argued, glancing at Kat, "but Katrina has all the qualifications I've been looking for. She's perfect for the job. I couldn't just let her walk back out the door."

Moss, Kat realized, would have done just that. She had the strong feeling he wanted to show her to the door.

"Have you told her what's been going on?"

The seemingly casual query brought a faint redness to Mark's finely formed features. "Most of it." He looked at Kat as if seeking confirmation.

Without thinking, she automatically rushed to his aid. "Mark has explained—"

She never got to finish. The intense gray eyes swerved her way, stopping her in mid-sentence. Swallowing dryly, Kat felt like a mouse suddenly faced with a dangerous predator who might or might not decide to pursue. She was so flustered by the intensity of that stare, she didn't even hear what the two men were saying until Mark's voice cut through her confusion.

"... were just finishing up anyway. Sounds good to me. What do you say, Katrina? TJ's is only a couple of blocks away."

"TJ's?" It came out as a breathless croak. Moss had straightened from the door, and he looked even taller and stronger than she remembered. Her attention swiveled away from his unsettling presence back to Mark's safe, friendly face.

"A local watering hole," he explained. "It's been a long day. How about a quick drink before you head home? Moss says he's buying." He shot his brother a wry look that, for all their obvious differences, spoke of deep affection. "For a change."

A refusal hovered on Kat's lips. If it had been just Mark, she wouldn't have hesitated. She already knew him well enough to know what to expect from the casual invitation. Moss was something else again. Him, she didn't trust an inch. Every time he looked at her she had the feeling she was in imminent danger of being either ravished or strangled—she couldn't decide which.

Unfortunately, both men seemed to take her hesitation for assent. While Mark called out for them to go on ahead and walked back into the studio for his jacket, Moss pushed open the door, motioning for her to precede him. He was acting, Kat decided irritably, as if her following him twice in one day was more danger than he cared to deal with.

"After you, shortstuff," he murmured.

Just the way he said it made Kat want to throw something at him.

TJ's turned out to be a cozy, attractive bar with a definite San Francisco flair. It was the kind of place, Kat reflected, she never would have patronized while married to Derek. Being a clear-cut case of snobbery on the hoof, her ex-husband wouldn't have liked the atmosphere—noisy and raucous—the decor—informal and generally less than elegant, unless you considered brass spittoons the height of elegance—or the patrons. Kat decided she emphatically liked all three.

What she wasn't sure she liked, however, was the way Moss Adams kept looking her over, as if he couldn't quite believe his good fortune at seeing her again. Or was he simply trying to figure out how to exact payment for the damage she'd done to his car?

When they reached a vacant corner booth, Kat innocently assumed Mark would slide in after her. Instead, a bland-looking Moss gently shouldered him aside and seated his long-limbed frame beside her, forcing Mark to sit opposite them. Kat couldn't have felt more trapped if a two-ton granite boulder had been placed across the exit.

Obviously surprised himself, Mark shot his brother a wary look as he raised his arm to catch the attention of a miniskirted waitress. "What will you have to drink, Katrina?"

Aware of Moss's hot gray eyes on her, Kat decided to exercise caution and ordered a Perrier and lime. Both brothers settled for draft beers, and while the drinks were being served, Mark slipped off his elegantly tailored jacket and started to loosen his blue silk tie. Then Moss said, with disarmingly casual interest, "When are you supposed to call Pederson?"

Kat, nervously twisting the stem of her glass, jerked to sudden attention. She didn't care how innocent Moss looked. She knew, she just *knew*—as sure as God made little green apples, and red ones, too, for that matter—that he was up to something.

Mark, on the other hand, who was either less suspecting than she was or just didn't know his own brother as well as Kat thought he should have, merely blinked at Moss and said, "What?"

"Pederson," Moss repeated. "At the advertising agency."

Mark looked blank, then chagrined. "Pederson," he echoed in obvious dismay. "Lord, I forgot all about it. I told him I'd call around five. What time is it?"

"Fifteen after."

Mark grimaced. "Maybe I'd better call him tomorrow."

"He's flying to France tomorrow. You need the account or not?"

By this time Kat had guessed that Moss was in the process of getting rid of Mark so they could be alone. Annoyed at the obvious ease with which he was manipulating his brother, she gave him a stony stare before turning to Mark.

"Why don't you call him from here?" she suggested.

She knew exactly what kind of adversary she was dealing with when Moss, again casually, informed her, "There's no phone here. Jake, the owner, hates the contraptions."

Which was obviously why he'd suggested this bar.

Kat could see Mark's indecision. He knew he should make the call but was obviously reluctant to leave. Maybe he knew Moss well enough after all, she thought with black amusement.

Finally he opened his mouth. But before he could say anything Moss interjected smoothly, "Don't worry about your new secretary. This'll give us a chance to get better acquainted, since I wasn't around earlier. I'll see her back to her car when we're through."

Get better acquainted? Kat sat up in alarm. What exactly did that mean? Her eyes flew to Mark in question.

"Moss is responsible for security now," he explained almost apologetically. "He usually interviews job applicants with me before I hire them. I suppose it's only fair to give him a chance to talk to you now, but don't feel you're being put on the spot in any way. Consider it a very informal interview. As far as I'm concerned, you've already got the job."

Fleetingly, Kat wondered why she didn't feel particularly reassured. And what did "responsible for security" mean?

"You don't mind giving me a few minutes of your time, do you, Ms. Langley?" Moss Adams asked with what Kat considered suspect politeness.

Pulling at the tattered remnants of her composure, she said—firmly she hoped—"No, of course not." If she'd been asked by anyone else, she'd have been sure of that, but since it was Moss . . .

Mark rose. "I guess I'll leave you to it, then. Call me tonight, will you, Moss? See you tomorrow, Katrina." He threw her an encouraging smile.

Unencouraged, Kat had to forcibly restrain her dismay as Mark, oblivious to the silent plea in her green eyes to stay, excused himself and grabbing his jacket, departed.

The silence left in Mark's wake positively crackled with electricity. Kat's whole body vibrated with it. So far, despite the bomb Mark had dropped about the typewriter, she'd been telling herself she had nothing to worry about as she pursued her investigation. Nothing to worry about? Moss Adams could give her a heart attack without even trying. No one, except Derek, had ever made her so aware of herself as a woman. No one, including Derek, had ever made her heart pound the way Moss Adams did every time he looked at her. Mark was a spring lamb in comparison.

Moss was definitely not a lamb.

Like diamonds and ice, he was full of sharp edges. A tough man. A rugged man. With an angular face and a nose that looked as if it had been broken once, perhaps in a fight. Yes, Kat decided, she could imagine him in a fight. She could imagine him doing *anything*.

"Stop looking so nervous," he chided as he stretched his long legs out under the small table and made himself more comfortable. "Even if I was annoyed at you for rearranging my car's bumper, what could happen to you in the middle of a public restaurant?"

"With you," Kat muttered, "who knows?" Swallowing hard, she studied the man next to her and wished she hadn't worn the wool dress, even if its copper shade did complement her coloring. It was hard to look cool, calm, and collected when the high, scratchy collar insisted on clinging damply to her throat. "That was very smooth just now. Mark never suspected a thing. Do you always find it so easy to manipulate situations to your own liking?"

Moss smiled unrepentantly. "Are you objecting to my technique or to me in general?"

Both. Mark she could handle. Moss was a different proposition altogether. "I was wondering why you went to so much trouble to get rid of Mark."

Moss picked up his frosted beer mug and raised his tawny eyebrows at her. "Because I didn't want him to hear what I have to say to you, of course."

She was afraid he'd say that. Kat's warning systems jangled into full red alert as all sorts of crazy notions about what Moss could possibly have to say to her that Mark shouldn't hear zigzagged through her mind. She didn't like even one of them. There were at least two sides to the complicated man before her, and she suspected she was presently facing the shrewd one. The ruthless one. The one who would strangle her if he knew what she was up to at his brother's studio. Moss was in charge of security. And she had just breached it by getting herself hired under false pretenses.

"I know we didn't settle it before," Kat said, determined to channel the conversation away from the subject of her employment, "but I plan to take full financial responsibility for the damage I did to your car—"

"Forget the car. That's not why I wanted to talk to you. We're supposed to be getting better acquainted. Remember?"

Kat didn't like the way he said that. "How much better?"

For a moment the heat returned to his gaze, and Kat knew he was thinking of their earlier meeting, as she was. "Don't look so worried." He squeezed her hand, briefly enveloping it in his distinctly larger one. "I just wanted to ask you a few questions. How much has Mark told you about the problems he's been having?"

Kat stared at her tingling fingers. "He said he's had some trouble keeping a secretary," she finally managed.

"Trouble," said Moss dryly, "is something of an understatement. Did he tell you how many secretaries have worked for him in the last four months?"

"Well, not exactly. But—"

"Ten. Three of them didn't last a week. Do you know why?"

Kat tried to keep too much interest from her voice. "Mark mentioned some accidents. Do you know what's causing all the problems?" She held her breath, waiting for his answer.

"If I knew that, sweetheart, you and I wouldn't be having this conversation."

Blushing at the casual endearment, Kat decided to get down to brass tacks. "Enlighten me, Mr. Adams. Why *are* we having this conversation?"

He considered her until it was all Kat could do not to squirm under the warmly assessing survey. "If I have to explain that to you, shortstuff, you're not half as smart as I think you are. My brother aside, not all men like dimwitted women. Are you being deliberately obtuse?"

Feeling like an idiot, Kat smiled brightly and reminded herself that while he might not like dimwitted women, he probably didn't appreciate independent ones, either. "Obtuse? What do you mean?"

"I'm trying to tell you this job you've just taken might be dangerous and that you'd be wise to go someplace else to work. Tell me something. Do you see yourself as some sort of heroine?"

Kat's laugh was short and honest. "Good grief, no."

"Then why take a job working for someone you know is having more than his share of problems?"

Why indeed? Kat was beginning to feel she'd inadvertently stepped into quicksand. She obviously couldn't tell Moss the truth—that she wasn't a secretary at all but a private investigator who needed to prove her competence; that she needed a decent case with a satisfying resolution or she'd be batting her head against the wall, forever doomed to boring cases while the plum jobs went to the men in her field—so she told him the next best thing. A half-truth.

"Because I need the money. And this job pays very well."

She hadn't exactly intended to enlist his sympathy with her supposed plight, which was just as well, since it wasn't forthcoming.

"It pays well for a reason," he pointed out. "It's known

as combat pay. Don't you think it might be smart to avoid potential trouble and try working elsewhere?"

Kat wondered if by "potential trouble" he meant himself. Mark had indicated the job itself wasn't dangerous, but he hadn't made the same claim about his brother.

"Mark doesn't seem to think the job is dangerous," she parried.

"Mark," said his brother, "wouldn't know danger if it hit him on the head. That's why I'm here. You know, most women would take this kind of warning seriously and hightail it."

"I'm not most women," Kat retorted before she could stop herself.

Moss nodded in wry agreement. "Damned right, you're not. You're a lot smarter, a lot sassier, and ten times more stubborn than most."

Kat smiled sweetly. "I'm sorry I don't live *down* to your expectations," she replied.

"You look sorry." Moss sipped his beer, watching her over the rim of the frosted mug. "Why do I get the feeling that the more I try to convince you to leave Mark's employ, the more determined you are to stay?"

"Why are you so determined to get me to leave?" Kat countered.

She knew she was in trouble when he smiled and said obligingly, "Because you're careless and hotheaded, and in my experience the combination is deadly."

"I am *not* careless!" Kat denied hotly, unintentionally demonstrating that at least one of the accusations was true. "Just because I hit your car—" She stopped as Moss pulled a slip of paper from his shirt pocket and held it out between two tanned fingers.

"What do you call this?"

"My address?" Kat supplied helpfully, recognizing her own handwriting.

"Evidence," he corrected. "You gave your name, address, and telephone number to a complete stranger."

Kat stared at him in dismay. So she had. "If I promise to be more careful in the future, would you stop trying to get rid of me?"

"Nope."

"Why not?"

"Because you're a headache I don't happen to need right now. I don't have time to baby-sit you if the going gets rough."

Was *that* what this was all about? Kat didn't know whether she wanted to laugh or spit. Here she'd been thinking he was concerned for her welfare.

"This may come as a terrible shock to you," she said, ignoring the lazy way he was looking her over again, "but I don't need to be baby-sat. I stopped being afraid of the dark years ago."

"I had a feeling you might say that. You won't be leaving then?"

"Not unless Mark asks me to," Kat confirmed.

"In that case," Moss said, "I'd better give you the same warning I've given your numerous predecessors. Keep your eyes open, expect the unexpected, and report anything suspicious to me."

Kat gave him a bright, hopeful smile. "Does this mean you've given up trying to get rid of me, then?"

"Hell, no." He bopped her gently but reprovingly on the nose with his knuckle, sending a whole new set of electrical impulses romping through her body. "It means I'm conceding this round to you because you earned it. But the battle is still raging, and this is one war I intend to win. I hope we understand each other, shortstuff."

The trouble was, of course, she didn't understand him at all. Worse, she didn't understand herself, either. Because even though she knew it wasn't wise to make snap judgments—she'd decided soon after meeting Derek they were perfectly suited for each other, and look where *that* miscalculation had landed her—she already knew that Moss Adams was one man she definitely wanted to bump into again.

CHAPTER
Four

STANDING IN HER sunny orange-and-yellow kitchen, Kat buttered an English muffin and tried to figure out just what, exactly, Moss Adams had meant by that last comment. She'd spent a sleepless night mulling it over, and it still wasn't clear in her mind.

Had he or had he not declared war on her? And if he had, what kind? Never mind that tangling with him on any level both excited and dismayed her, she was supposed to be investigating the goings-on at Mark Adams's studio, not engaging in a personal battle of the sexes with the owner's brother. She needed him focusing his attention on her like she needed a hole in the head. What if he didn't play by the rules? What if the skirmishes between them—and somehow she knew there would be more of them—got very physical indeed?

"Are you planning on buttering that thing all morning?"

At the sound of her brother's amused voice, Kat turned. Slightly taller, hair a little browner, but with the same gray-green eyes and straight nose, Ken—visually—was the male version of herself. In personality, however, he was something else again. "You know," he said conversationally as he sauntered toward the refrigerator, "most people put the butter *under* the jam, not on top of it."

Grimacing at the mess in her hand, Kat dumped it into the trash and eyed her brother as he raided her icebox. "Don't you ever eat your own food? My grocery bill doubles every time you visit me."

"Goodness, we *did* get up on the wrong side of the bed this morning, didn't we?" Ken poured himself some orange juice. "I guess that explains the outfit you've got on."

Kat frowned at her carefully chosen ensemble. "What's wrong with it?"

"What's right with it?"

"It's brand-new!"

"That's no excuse." Ken wrinkled his nose—so like Kat's own—in distaste. "What the hell do you call that color?"

"For an artist, you're remarkably ignorant. It's teal blue. Or is it teal green? No matter," Kat decided, "I'm going to be perfectly coordinated with the office furnishings."

"Is that what you want? To blend in with the furniture?"

"In this case"—Kat thought of Moss and felt her heart hopscotch—"yes. I'm undercover, remember? Will you stop frowning like that?"

"I can't help it. That suit makes you look like a—"

"Secretary?" Kat supplied hopefully.

"I was going to say *grandmother* until I remembered you can outwrestle me." Dodging a flying muffin, Ken peered back over the refrigerator door. "So you convinced Mark Adams to hire you, did you? Don't tell me you did the improbable and actually arrived on time?"

"Look who's talking!" Ken was as punctual as Kat was. The difference was that Ken's lateness apparently didn't bother him at all, while Kat's habitual tardiness was something she was forever battling—without much success.

"Arriving fashionably late is part of the artistic temperament. How's the investigation going?" Ken rummaged deeper in the icebox.

Thinking of her nerve-racking talk with Moss Adams, Kat sighed. "Things could be better. Exactly how much do you know about Mark Adams and what's been going on at his studio?"

Ken pulled a bowl of fruit from the refrigerator. "All I know is what I hear. We've used some of the same models." He popped a berry into his mouth. "If you want firsthand information, why don't you try talking to his last secretary?"

"Lisa Dawson? Can't. She's currently vacationing in the wilds of Colorado, recovering, I'm told, from her near-electrocution. You know, other than what happened to her, I'm still not sure why everyone seems so anxious to stampede. Especially the models. I mean, someone replacing your prized Gucci shoes with dime-store originals might give you blisters and a case of bad temper, and discovering that your strapless size thirty-four-A bra has suddenly become a forty-six triple-D cup would be frustrating, but it all sounds more disruptive than dangerous. Something a practical joker might dream up. Hardly threatening enough to cause mass hysteria."

Ken shrugged. "You have to understand models. Their looks are everything. What threatens that, threatens them. What do you think of Mark Adams?"

"He's cute. Nice. Naive. He seems to think what's happening is all sort of a bad coincidence. Do you know if he's married?"

"Haven't the foggiest. Why, interested in him?"

Kat shook her head. "He's not my type." She tried not to think of Moss, who she was very much afraid *was* her type.

"Anything interesting happen while you were there yesterday?" Slathering butter on two more muffins, Ken handed her one.

Kat bit into it, thought about Moss again, and smiled. "That depends on what you consider interesting."

"Ask a stupid question . . . You know, I still think you shouldn't have touched this job with a ten-foot pole. Just because you're having a little trouble getting cases—"

"A *little* trouble!"

"Okay, okay, so things have been tough for you since you started the agency. You'll get more and better cases eventually," Ken assured her with all the confidence of the truly unknowledgeable.

"I'll get more and better cases," Kat retorted, "when people start taking me seriously. And why am I letting you drag me into this conversation? I thought we'd agreed we wouldn't discuss this case."

"You agreed. I didn't. That look on your face already has me wishing I'd never opened my mouth about Mark Adams or his studio. What if you get hurt again?"

Kat raised her eyes heavenward. "Will you stop worrying already? Everything is working out like I'd hoped." If you discounted Moss Adams, of course. "It's always easier to work a case like this from the inside. I've got access to Mark's files, and if anything else funny happens, I'll be right there to see it." With, in all probability, Moss breathing down her neck.

"That's supposed to make me stop worrying?"

Kat sighed in exasperation. "Come on, Kenny. I'm talking about investigating what joker substituted tear gas for fake smoke, not an unsolved murder. Do you really think I would have taken this case if I thought it might be the least bit dangerous?"

"Yes!" While Kat winced at the vehemence in that one word, he went on, "You know, just because you have a black belt in karate—"

"Brown," Kat corrected automatically, idly wondering if Moss Adams had any training in martial arts.

"Whatever." Ken waved an impatient hand. "The point is, you're not indestructible. From what I've heard, every secretary who's worked there during the last six months has had reason to regret it."

Yes, Kat wondered, but *why* have they regretted it?

"I'm almost embarrassed to tell you," Kim Lambertson admitted over coffee half an hour later. "It all sounds so melodramatic. I can understand your interest, of course. As long as you're working for Mark, you ought to know what to expect. The problem is, I don't really know that much.

I wasn't there for very long," she explained, biting into a jelly doughnut.

Kat smiled in understanding at Lisa Dawson's predecessor and the only one of Mark Adams's secretaries to stay over a week and a half. "Why don't you start by telling me why you left?" she suggested.

The chubby blonde turned pink. "Someone tampered with my chair. At least," she temporized, wiping her fingers on a napkin, "I think they did. Mark didn't seem to think the back falling clean off was all that unusual, but since it happened two days after the fire—"

"Fire?" Kat repeated, her interest perking.

"That's how it starts, you see. First there's a small fire in the office, sort of like a warning; then something else strange happens, like with my chair. Kelly, the girl before me, almost got beaned by a ceiling tile falling on her desk. She quit on her second day," Kim added.

"Had there been a fire that time, too?"

"Oh, sure. Behind the file cabinet. I heard it took Mark a good fifteen minutes to put that one out. But that was nothing, apparently, compared to the one in the bathroom the time before. That nearly burned the place down. You know, if I were you, I'd find a job somewhere else. Nobody seems to know who's doing these crazy things or why, but like I told that humongous brother of Mark's—"

"Brother?" Kat felt her heart skip a beat.

The blonde grimaced. "Mark is sweet, but that brother of his is enough to make Mark's secretaries leave, pronto. After a grilling by him I felt like the number one suspect in an ax murder. Take my word for it, you'd be better off someplace else. In any case, be on the lookout. Especially if there happens to be another fire."

The first things Kat noticed when she arrived at the office—only ten minutes late—were Laurel Tandy and the bouquet of long-stemmed red roses, both sitting on her desk.

Dressed in an eye-opening animal-print jumpsuit and reclined into what Kat imagined was feline repose, the pencil-thin model sat up and sighed as Kat rushed through the door. "Thank goodness, you're back. I was afraid Mark would have me answering the phone again today."

Kat grimaced. "If I'd gotten here any later," she said, hanging up her jacket and approaching the desk, "you probably would be."

"Are you kidding?" Laurel laughed. "Even if he were a stickler for promptness, which he's not, and were already here, which he isn't, Mark's too nice to fire you. Ah, that reminds me."

Kat was just beginning to wonder how Laurel Tandy had managed to enter the building before Mark's arrival when the other woman dug into her canvas tote and produced an envelope.

"Here." She handed it to Kat. "Mark's brother asked me to give this to you when he let me in this morning. Knowing him, it's probably a questionnaire."

Opening the envelope, Kat read the note inside with its boldly scrawled *Dinner tonight?* and felt her blood quicken.

"How Mark and that man could be related," Laurel said, shaking her head, "is beyond me. How did you do yesterday?"

Pocketing the piece of paper, Kat dropped her purse into a desk drawer. "Well, after getting yelled at by Frank Morgan—"

The dark-haired model made a moue. "There are nice agency heads, and there are not-so-nice ones. Guess which category dear old Frank falls into?" Flicking a minuscule piece of lint from her slender thigh, she asked with open curiosity, "Did he have reason to yell? Or was he just being his pleasant self?"

Thinking of Lisa Dawson, Kat slowly uncovered the typewriter, looking for signs of tampering. "I gathered he was annoyed that the ring Emma Li needed for the Anson's Jewelers ad disappeared during a shoot last week. He said it wasn't the first time a model of his had had trouble like that here, but he indicated it might very well be the last. Does that sort of thing happen often?"

"What? The yelling? Or a model losing something?"

Kat surreptitiously checked her chair. "Both."

Laurel shrugged. "When I was playing secretary for Mark, it happened maybe four or five times. I swear, some of my cohorts have nothing but empty space between their ears. You'll see what I mean when you meet Candy-Anna," she added with a sigh.

"What happens when a model loses something needed for a shoot?" Kat kept her voice casual, aware she was treading a fine line between natural curiosity and suspicious interest.

The model lifted her thin shoulders again. "Depends. If the poor girl has simply misplaced it, people tap their feet impatiently until it's found. If she's truly lost it, Mark might try to get a replacement. If worse comes to worst, he reschedules the shoot." She frowned at the wall clock. "Gad, I'm late for a shoot myself. Anything I can help you with before I scoot?"

Kat gave a chagrined smile. "Well, actually, I was wondering . . . Should I run for cover if anything gets lost? I imagine Mark must get tired of that sort of thing. What does he do? Yell a lot?"

Laurel slid off Kat's desk. "You must be joking. Mark wouldn't have the heart to chew out Jack the Ripper. He never yells, though he's surely had cause. Especially lately." She shook her head and sympathized, "Poor Carol. I hear she positively freaked out when her tiger tooth lucky charm turned up missing that time. Of course, Mark was a dear about the whole thing, knowing how much it meant to her. A shame he lost the account she'd been doing with him, though. But goodness knows, Carol was hardly eager to come back for another shoot, considering all that's been going on."

"I understand from what Mark was saying, a number of strange things have been happening around here. Doesn't it make you nervous?" Kat did her best to look nervous herself.

"Me? Naw. I'm not a worrier. Besides, I've been lucky"— the model rapped her knuckles lightly on the wooden doorjamb—"so far. By the way, those came for you a little while ago." She nodded toward the flowers and gave Kat a wink as she swayed out the door.

There was no card. Wondering if she was being paranoid, Kat had just finished establishing that they weren't booby-trapped and was making guesses about who'd sent the sweetly pungent bouquet when Mark, looking trim and elegant in a pin-striped suit, appeared in the doorway with a willowy brunette on his arm.

"Ah, Katrina," he said, striding lithely into the room, "you've returned. I was hoping you would." He gave the gorgeous creature next to him an indulgent smile. "Katrina, you haven't met Candy-Anna Carpenter yet, have you? She's new, but she's already one of the hottest tickets in town. Candy, this is Katrina, my new secretary. Say hello, dear."

"Hello," the model said obediently, eyeing first the flowers and then Kat.

"And stop coveting the roses," Mark scolded before turning back to Kat. "Not very imaginative, I know, but the florist assured me I couldn't go wrong with them. Hope he was right."

Vaguely disappointed they were from Mark and not Moss, Kat smiled brightly. "I doubt there's a woman on earth who doesn't love roses. They're beautiful. Thank you."

"I'm an orchid girl myself." The brunette aimed the heavy-handed hint squarely at Mark. "I just love the way they smell." She turned big brown eyes to Kat. "Don't you?"

Kat looked blankly at Mark.

"Orchids don't have any fragrance," he said kindly to Candy-Anna.

"Oh." The young model looked nonplussed. "Don't they?"

Mark, rolling his eyes, shooed her into the studio and turned back to Kat. "You do like roses, don't you?"

Kat smiled in puzzlement. "Of course, but what's the occasion?"

"How did your interview with Moss go?" he asked. When Kat wrinkled her nose involuntarily, he admitted, "That's the occasion. I hope he wasn't too hard on you. He's not very happy about my hiring another secretary. He wanted me to wait until things had settled down a little more."

It struck Kat that "not very happy" was a mild way to describe Moss's reaction to her employment. Something must have shown on her face, she realized ruefully, because Mark's hazel eyes sharpened. "Was he that rough on you? Should I have bought two dozen roses?"

A denial sprang to Kat's lips, but at the last minute she changed her mind. Why lie? She couldn't think of one reason why she should try to defend Moss, who could plainly look after himself. "I got the impression your brother wasn't exactly thrilled to have me working here," she conceded.

Mark sighed. "I hate to ask, but I will. What did he say?" As he spoke, he shed his jacket, revealing a silk shirt and tie.

Smoothing her skirt, Kat hesitated before answering. She didn't want to cause a rift between them, but if Mark could put even a *little* restraint on his sibling, it would certainly make her job easier. "He seems to think I'm in danger," she said, doing her best to appear worried. "He suggested I look for work elsewhere."

"Did he?" Mark looked annoyed. "I'm sorry, Katrina. I should have warned you that Moss doesn't mince words. Don't pay any attention to him. I know he's somewhat intimidating, but I assure you his bark is worse than his bite."

"I'll try to remember that," Kat said dryly.

A look of understanding shot between them. "Moss is something of a loner," Mark conceded, folding his jacket carefully over his arm. "Don't be surprised if he doesn't spend much time with conventional small talk. He's not much of a social animal."

Kat nodded. Small talk was the last thing she would have expected from Moss. And a social animal was the last thing she would have called him. An animal, perhaps, but hardly a social one.

"You said he's in charge of security," she said, carefully broaching the subject that really concerned her, "but I got the feeling he hasn't always been. Is he helping you out on a temporary basis?" If she was lucky, he'd have to return soon to his normal occupation, whatever it was. Then she could proceed unhindered with her investigation.

"Moss doesn't have what you'd call a regular job," Mark replied, dashing her hopes, "so I guess he'll stay as long as he's needed. I suppose you could call him a free-lancer," he added thoughtfully.

I could call him a lot of things, Kat thought. Too smart, too shrewd, the most persistent man she'd ever met...

"He prefers to work as a sort of trouble-shooter with private companies," Mark elaborated, "helping them set up security systems."

Trouble-shooter? Kat gave a silent snort. Troublemaker was more like it. "Do you expect him to stay indefinitely then?" she asked. Please say no.

Mark shook his head. "Probably not. He's a damned fine private investigator. It's been a difficult case so far, but if anyone can solve it, he can. I don't expect it'll take too much longer."

At first Kat was certain she hadn't heard right. Moss was a private investigator? No, he couldn't be. Could he? She'd assumed—no, hoped—he was some sort of amateur sleuth. Lord, this was all she needed! No wonder he seemed so suspicious!

Mark looked as if he expected her to say something, so Kat picked the first thing that popped into her head. "It sounds like a dangerous profession. His wife must be very understanding."

"Oh, Moss isn't married." Mark paused. "He's not exactly... well, fond of the fairer sex."

Kat stared at him. Not fond of women? Are we talking about the same man? she wondered wildly. Moss Adams might not look like the type who went for women, especially independent redheads who bashed into his car, but beneath that cool exterior the man was a raving sex maniac. She was sure of it.

This time Mark looked as if he hoped Kat wouldn't pursue the subject. She didn't. Busy planning the next step in her investigation, she told herself she couldn't care less what Moss Adams liked or disliked about her or any other woman, as long as he stayed at least twenty feet away from her at all times.

He didn't, of course.

CHAPTER
Five

A KEY TO the studio had become hers just for the asking, and she'd managed to avoid Moss all morning. Pleased with how things were proceeding so far, Kat was precariously balanced on tiptoe on the highest rung of the five-step wooden ladder, checking out the skylight Mark had assured her was next to impossible to open for ventilation—or possible entry?—when the door opened. Half expecting it to be Mark returning early from lunch, she turned with a ready explanation for her rather unsecretarial behavior on her lips . . . and froze.

"Hello, shortstuff. Still here, I see."

Eyeing her arch-rival warily from her perch, Kat silently took in the tan corduroy jeans and burgundy V-necked sweater intimately hugging Moss Adams's lean, long-limbed body and wondered how he could look so devastatingly sexy without even trying.

"Mark's not in," she told him in an abortive attempt at nonchalance. Somehow, she realized, she'd managed to sound even more nervous than she felt. And more guilty.

Moss smiled. "No problem. You're the one I wanted to talk to."

She was afraid he'd say that.

Taking a deep breath, Kat wondered fleetingly if Moss had purposely waited for Mark to leave so he could catch her alone. Quickly deciding that he was more than capable of such sneaky maneuvering, she momentarily abandoned her examination of the skylight and surveyed him with extreme caution as he approached her desk and seated himself on the edge.

"Mind telling me what you've been up to today?"

As seemed to be his habit, he'd shoved the sleeves of his pullover sweater up to his elbows. But even though his tanned, muscled forearms were crossed lazily over his broad chest, even though he appeared perfectly relaxed, Kat had the distinct impression he was holding back the impulse to throttle her. Which probably meant, she concluded, that he'd spotted the scraps of electrical cord and the two-pronged plug she'd discarded in the wastebasket.

Wishing she weren't *quite* so pleased to see him when she knew his presence meant nothing but trouble for her, Kat answered, "If you must know, I replaced the plug on the coffeepot. The cord was frayed at the end." Constituting a possible fire hazard, she could have added, but didn't. She wasn't even sure why she'd checked the cord on the coffee maker before plugging it in. She supposed Moss's dire warnings of danger were lodged somewhere in the back of her mind, and having already seen Mark's habit of jerking it from the socket by the cord, she hadn't been overly surprised or particularly alarmed to find the plug damaged. All the same, considering Lisa Dawson's accident, she hadn't entirely ruled out the possibility of sabotage as she'd set to work mending it.

"I thought I asked you to report anything suspicious to me," Moss said mildly, picking up the open penknife on her desk and sheathing the blade with a quick snap.

Ignoring the tremor of alarm flickering down her spine, Kat gave him a brightly naive smile. "What, pray tell, is so suspicious about a frayed cord?"

"If you'd been here longer," he assured her, crossing his long legs to expose polished ankle-high boots, "you wouldn't ask. Come across anything else that looks like it might be trouble?"

"Besides you, you mean? Not really." She watched him settle himself more comfortably on her desk. He looked like a man with no immediate plans for leaving, she realized in dismay, and she was sure she knew why. "You know, if you've come to try to talk me into quitting again, don't waste your time."

Smiling with unexpected charm, Moss lifted his large hands in patently insincere denial. "Would I do that?" As Kat let out a barely stifled snort, he said idly, "By the way, I understand Mark gave you a key to the studio today. I'd like it back, please."

Kat didn't even bother asking how he knew about the key; she simply dug it out and, with a look that would have shriveled a lesser man, dropped it into his extended palm. Sliding the key into his pants pocket, Moss carefully lifted one of the flowers Mark had given her and studied the scarlet bloom for a moment. "Did you, by any chance, tell Mark about our conversation yesterday?"

Kat's left eyebrow rose. "Of course. Did you think I wouldn't?"

Moss twirled the rose between his fingers. "What did he say?"

Kat smiled down at him with ill-disguised satisfaction. "He told me not to pay any attention to you," she confided. "That your bark is worse than your bite."

Moss looked amused. "Did he indeed? And did you believe him?"

Something in the softly worded query goaded her into saying flippantly, "Naturally. After all, he's the one who hired me, isn't he? I have no reason to fault his judgment."

The molten gray eyes shifted from the flower to her face, sending heat impulses right down to Kat's toes. "I hope you don't have any aspirations where Mark is concerned," he said in gentle warning. "You'd be wasting your time. Even if he went for hotheads, he never mixes business and pleasure. At least, not for long."

Stunned by her soul-rocking reaction to the hot-eyed caress, Kat struggled for control as she said smartly, "And what about you, Mr. Adams? Do you ever mix business and pleasure? Or are you too busy minding other people's business to have time for the latter?"

Kat had meant it as a put-down, not a come-on. She was appalled when Moss chose to put his own design on the careless words. "Like most people, I manage to squeeze in both, shortstuff. What did you have in mind?"

Not what he clearly did! Searching for a suitably ego-flattening retort, Kat finally gave up and went back to her inspection of the skylight. Moss sighed audibly. "I'm sure I'm going to regret asking, but would you mind telling me what the hell you're doing up there?"

Wouldn't he like to know! "What does it look like I'm doing?"

"Asking for trouble. Tell me something. Do you go out of your way for opportunities to stick your neck out, or do the ideas for stunts like this pop spontaneously into that pretty head of yours?"

His voice warned her not to answer that, even if his expression hadn't, but Kat was too irritated with the crazy way her heart had suddenly begun to pound to take heed. "I'm not putting myself in any danger," she insisted, ignoring the slowly rising tawny eyebrow.

"That ladder is unstable," Moss pointed out calmly.

So is my nervous system! Kat decided. "It's stuffy in here. I thought it might help to to open this up," she lied.

"Come on down, and I'll do it for you."

Kat stared at his proffered hand. He had such large hands. Such strong hands. Remembering the feel of them on her neck in the shopping center parking lot, she swallowed dryly. "I'm not helpless."

"No," Moss agreed, "you're just too stubborn for your own good."

Which was perceptive of him but annoying all the same.

"You should talk." Stretching, she pushed harder on the window latch to see if it would give.

Moss got up to steady the ladder as it wobbled slightly beneath her high-heeled feet. "Have you got a death wish?"

Kat smiled brightly down at him. "No, do you?"

She hadn't exactly expected him to cower under the implied warning, but she didn't expect the disarming smile, either.

"Are you threatening me?"

Kat turned innocent eyes on him. "Are you feeling threatened?"

"No, just thwarted. You're sure one aggressive lady, aren't you?"

"I think the word you're looking for," Kat supplied kindly, "is *liberated*."

"Sassy as hell, too. I don't know why I keep trying to save your neck."

"I don't know why, either. Why don't you stop?"

"I keep asking myself the same thing. Are you coming down or not?"

"Not," Kat decided. "I have my womanly pride to consider."

"I was more worried about your neck. How do you suppose I'm going to feel if you go and kill yourself?"

"Relieved?" Kat guessed.

"You don't know me very well. You know, as long as you're my responsibility, the least you could do is try to cooperate."

He couldn't have chosen better words to raise her ire if he'd tried. "Will you please stop acting as if I'm a piece of company property?" Kat exploded. "I'm not your responsibility; I'm responsible for myself!"

"Not as long as you're working for Mark, you're not. Are you always this emotional?"

"Are you always this *unemotional?*" Kat sniped.

His slow smile sent a flicker of purely female alarm skittering down her spine. "I'm not feeling particularly unemotional at the moment. In fact, with any encouragement from you at all, I suspect I could get downright excited.

Why don't you climb down from there," he suggested amiably, "before I'm forced to drag you down?"

"Touch me," Kat promised just as amiably, "and I'll break your arm. I don't know what you're so worried about," she added.

"You're going to fall."

"Oh, for goodness sake! I am *not*"—Kat waved her hand in growing impatience—"going to fall—"

She'd barely mouthed the words when she felt the ladder tilt dangerously. Wood cracked with an audible snap, the ladder swayed off-balance, and Kat, grasping in horror at nothing but empty air, fell . . . or started to. Fleetingly, she saw a blur of burgundy reaching up. A split second later, Moss's warm hands were spanning her rib cage, catching her in midair.

Too startled to speak, Kat found herself eyeball-to-eyeball with his molten-metal eyes. A flood of quicksilver rushed through her veins as the phrase "too close for comfort" took on a whole new meaning for her. Literally standing on his toes, she could feel every solid inch of his long-limbed body, see the small, pale scar beneath the tawny eyebrow, count every one of the dark, spiky lashes.

Her heart marched around inside her chest like a maniacal jackhammer on a rampage, but even in her less-than-lucid state of mind, Kat recognized that it wasn't fear turning her bones to pulp. It was sheer, unadulterated desire. Fighting for control, she struggled to pull air into her constricted lungs and felt her breasts touch his hard chest. Why didn't he do something? *Say* something?

After what seemed an eternity, he did both.

Kat stiffened involuntarily as Moss leaned forward, eliminating the millimeter of space between them, melding them together in an even more intimate embrace. Her eyes widening in distress as her whole body seemed to come alive, she felt the soft abrasion of his hard cheek touching hers, felt his breath warm on her skin, felt her own breath stop as he moved his body still closer to hers and whispered conspiratorially in her ear, "We've got to stop meeting like this, shortstuff."

For at least the second time since she'd met him, Kat
felt like a complete ninny. She'd thought he was going to
kiss her, dammit! Worse, she'd actually *wanted* him to.
Biting her lower lip, flailing around for something equally
flip to say, Kat was busy trying to figure out why sparring
with him turned her on so much when the quick tap of
approaching feet had them both turning around.

"Hey, you two." Candy-Anna's brown eyes were wide
with curiosity. "It's awfully quiet around here. Anybody
know where Mark is? I'm supposed to be doing the Fatima
spread right after lunch." Hefting her large canvas purse
onto her shoulder, she paused, finally noting their conspic-
uous closeness. "What are you guys doing there, anyway?"

Moss's reply was noncommittal. Kat couldn't have spoken if she'd tried.

"All right. Let's see some more leg. Good. Good." *Whirr.*
Whirr. "Look bitchy now. No, Candy, not apopletic. Bitchy.
That's right. Great." *Whirr. Whirr.* "Let's get you on the
bed now."

She simply had to get Moss off her mind. Sitting at her
desk, Kat listened to Mark encouraging Candy-Anna as his
Nikon captured the model's image for posterity, and tried
to concentrate on her investigation.

So far, she'd scoured the personnel files of Mark's former
employees and gone through the files of clients past and
present, looking for anything that might indicate that one
of them held a grudge against Mark. She'd even contacted
several of the modeling agencies Mark had worked with,
ostensibly to complete their files for a fictional audit. She'd
come up with exactly nothing.

Considering her actions in retrospect, Kat saw no fault
with her methods. Taking into account the basics of where
and when each act of sabotage had occurred, she'd systematically made up lists of possible suspects. She'd considered
deliverymen, mailmen, janitors—just about everyone who
had ever set foot on Mark Adam's property, including Mark
himself—and then eliminated possibility after possibility

for lack of motive or opportunity or both.

Kat sighed in frustration. For the first time since she'd begun her investigation, she was beginning to see what Moss was up against. The thought of being up against Moss, both literally as well as figuratively, snuck into Kat's mind. Forcefully pushing it aside, she listened to Mark coaxing Candy onto the red-satin-covered bed.

"Okay, now," she heard him say as strains of soft rock music drifted from the studio's tape deck, "pick up the fake snake and pretend you're going to kiss it."

Kat heard Candy's mumbled protest and Mark's patient answer, "I didn't say you had to kiss it. I said pretend you were going to. That's my girl. Just pick up the rubber snake and—"

Candy-Anna's shriek lifted Kat halfway off her swivel chair. Dropping her pen, Kat rushed into the adjoining studio. Her eyes landed on Candy-Anna, huddled fearfully in Mark's comforting embrace, and then on the small brown garter snake slithering across the studio floor.

"Now, Candy." Mark's consoling voice was nearly drowned out by the young model's snuffling. "It was only a little garden snake."

"I hate snakes!" She sobbed into his silk shirt. "They're horrible, disgusting, slimy—"

As the young girl gave a litany of the reptile's offenses, Kat grabbed a basket, dumped out the artificial daisies it held, and guided the snake into the receptacle while Mark, shooting a grateful look to her over Candy-Anna's bent head, escorted the model out of the studio.

Less than five minutes after Mark left to take the shuddering girl home, Kat, still wondering who had replaced the rubber version with the real item, returned from the entry garden, where she'd released the snake, and smelled smoke. At first she attributed the odor to Frank Morgan. An inveterate cigar smoker, the short, overweight head of the Morgan Modeling Agency had been in earlier to complain to Mark in person about Emma Li's missing ring, leaving a pungent trail behind him.

Kat sniffed the air again. Somehow, it didn't smell like Frank Morgan's awful rum-soaked stogie. It smelled, if possible, even worse.

Puzzled, she followed the odor across the studio to Mark's darkroom. Mark always closed the door of the cubicle behind him, and since no one else had had reason to enter, it remained shut. Feeling just a little paranoid after having talked with Kim Lambertson, Kat turned the knob and pushed the door open about a foot. Two seconds later, the smoke alarm above her head began screeching in warning as choking clouds of acrid black smoke, billowing ominously from the metal trash can, funneled toward her.

Kat automatically slammed the door shut, searched quickly around the prop-littered studio, and saw everything from bustles to stuffed mooseheads. Finally she spotted a fire extinguisher.

Holding her breath, she threw open the darkroom door and doused the smoldering wastebasket. It hissed and belched more smoke, but after a moment the fire was out. It hadn't been large to begin with, she realized, just incredibly smoky. When she peered into the can's soggy interior she knew why. Two of the four rolls of film Mark had expended earlier that day on Laurel Tandy had been burned.

So much for her sharp eyes and powers of observation, Kat decided in disgust, emerging from the darkroom. Not only had she missed whoever started the blaze, she'd allowed it to happen right under her nose. Sighing, she climbed onto a chair and removed the battery from the still-shrieking smoke alarm. Then, after opening the studio's three windows, she picked up a magazine and started fanning out the smoke.

Kat had the mess cleaned up before Mark returned from taking Candy-Anna home. The can of air freshener she'd emptied into the room masked most of the lingering odor of smoke, but unless Mark had developed a walloping head-cold during the interim, Kat didn't think for a minute he wouldn't notice the telltale fragrance of burning film. Sure enough, when Kat walked in to deliver a message, he was standing in the studio, sniffing the air in obvious puzzlement as he reloaded his camera.

"Am I imagining it"—he frowned at her—"or do I smell smoke?"

Kat had already decided that, since no harm had actually been done, there was no point in mentioning the small blaze. Eventually Mark would discover the film missing, but if she told him it had been burned, he would probably construe it as another suspicious incident and start to consider Moss's suggestion that he let her go for her own safety. And even though Kat fully suspected the fire *was* suspicious in origin, that was the last thing she wanted.

"Frank Morgan and his cigar were in earlier," she reminded him, feeling just a little guilty at the deception. The end justifies the means, she told herself—not for the first time—trying to believe it.

Mark seemed to accept the explanation without question, but Kat was sure Moss wouldn't. One look and those shrewd gray eyes would spot the blackened wastebasket and come to the appropriate conclusion. And he'd manage to use it against her.

Kat realized she couldn't possibly avoid a confrontation with Moss indefinitely, but she tried anyway. Ten minutes before he was due to check in at the office, she made sure she was elsewhere. She prolonged her afternoon break and ran every conceivable errand that would take her out of the office that afternoon. By the time she drove home she was a nervous wreck, trying to imagine the worst thing Moss could do to her when he finally caught up with her.

She was deeply asleep when the phone rang at her bedside. Dragging her eyelids open, Kat blearily focused on the digital alarm clock sitting on the nightstand. Disgusted, she reached out and groped for the shrilling receiver. Finding it in the dark, she lay back with it pressed to her ear. "Hello," she mumbled.

"You can't avoid me forever, shortstuff."

Kat's eyes flew open. She'd recognize that deep, unsettling purr anywhere, anytime, any hour. Struggling to a sitting position, she peered at her bedside clock again to make sure she wasn't imagining that it really was the middle of the night. She wasn't.

"Have you any idea what time it is?" she demanded, pulling the flowered sheet around her in irritation.

"No."

Moss's unrepentant tone indicated he didn't care, either, so Kat enlightened him. "It's two in the morning," she hissed into the yellow phone.

"Were you in bed?"

The insolence in the question made Kat snap, "I *am* in bed."

"Alone?"

Kat's hand tightened on the receiver at the husky query. "Have you got anything important to say before I hang up on you?"

Kat could have sworn there was a soft chuckle on the other end of the line. "Tell me what happened today," Moss purred, "and I'll let you go back to your sweet dreams."

There was something distinctly unsettling, Kat decided, about sitting in bed listening to that gravelly voice with nothing but a sheet and the darkness of night to cover her. She could almost imagine him propped up in his own bed, phone cradled on his bare, tanned shoulder, the sheets tucked around his equally bare lower body . . .

The vision was so sharp and so disturbing, Kat's mouth suddenly felt stuffed with cotton. What the dickens was she thinking? Licking her lips and forcing her attention to the matter at hand, she said airily, "I don't know what you're talking about."

"Do you want me to come over so we can discuss it in person?"

Kat hesitated at the softly spoken question. Did she? Now, that was an interesting thought. For a moment she imagined Moss standing next to her in her darkened bedroom, with only the soft gleam of moonlight illuminating his lean, bronzed body . . . She shook herself mentally. What on earth was she *doing*? "It's raining," she pointed out a little breathlessly. "You'd get wet and catch cold."

"Taking that to mean you just might be as concerned about my welfare as I am about yours," he purred into the phone, "why don't you tell me what happened today so we can both go back to sleep?"

Sighing up at her shadowed ceiling, Kat did. Briefly. Making no attempt to hide the fact that she thought he was making a mountain out of a very small molehill. In the pause that followed, she found herself again visualizing Moss, leaning back against the padded headboard beside her, his body teak-brown among the sleep-tossed yellow-and-white sheets. Somehow she just knew he didn't wear pajamas . . .

"Convinced yet that you'd be better off employed else-where?"

The soft question jarred her back to reality. Whether or not Moss wore sleepwear was irrelevant; his sole purpose in life seemed to be to curtail her employment at Mark's studio, and she'd better not forget it.

"Don't be ridiculous," she retorted, irritated at herself as much as at him. "There's a perfectly logical reason for these stupid accidents." She just wished she could name it! Annoyed at the way her heart was still tap-dancing at the sound of his voice, she added sweetly, "And I'm sure Mark will discover it even if you seem unable to."

Kat could have sworn there was amusement in Moss's reply as he said complacently, "I'm sure Mark would find your faith in him infinitely reassuring. Just as I'm sure he believed your explanation for the fire today. What did he say, by the way?"

Feeling like a rabbit who'd just stepped into a trap, Kat bit her lower lip. "Didn't you two discuss it?" she hedged.

"I haven't talked to him yet. What did he say about the fire, shortstuff?"

There it was again. That almost tangible caress in his deep voice when he called her that ridiculous name. Did he know how her pulse started to hammer when he talked to her like that?

Clearing her throat, Kat tried to pull herself together. "I haven't told Mark yet," she conceded, knowing it was useless to lie. He'd see straight through anything but the truth.

"Were you going to?"

The pause lengthened. Kat already knew the answer to that and so, she suspected, did he.

"No," she admitted, "I thought he'd only worry."

"Maybe he ought to worry a little more," Moss observed mildly. "It might be better for everyone involved if he took this whole thing more seriously."

Kat closed her eyes, fighting the feeling of dejection settling over her. "I suppose this means you're going to tell him," she managed finally, unable to disguise her bitterness. It had been an intriguing case. While it had lasted.

Kat heard a sigh from his end of the line. Of regret? Or simply impatience?

"I don't really have any choice, honey," he said gently. "I was hired to look out for Mark's interests. Try not to take it personally."

"How can I not take it personally?" Kat demanded, suddenly angry with him. How dare he sound almost regretful when, at the same time, he was about to ruin her life? "Dammit, you know that fire wasn't my fault!"

"An accident doesn't have to be your fault," Moss pointed out with irrefutable logic, "to kill you. Leave while you still can, Kat. You might think you have nine lives, but it's not wise to tempt fate."

Gently replacing the receiver, Kat wondered if it might not be equally unwise to tempt Moss. And what would happen to a woman who dared.

CHAPTER
Six

3:31. 3:32. 3:33. Kat buried her head under the pillow and willed herself to go back to sleep. Finally throwing off the insomnia-rumpled sheets, she slid off the bed and headed for the bathroom. She might as well face it. After talking to Moss, her mind as well as her heart had shifted into high gear, and there was no way she was going to get any more sleep that night. She might as well do something constructive. It took her all of two seconds to come up with a suitable project.

With her car in the body shop for repairs, Kat had plenty of time to develop a plan of action as she pedaled her bike across town. Careful not to attract attention, she parked her ten-speed just inside the wrought-iron fence and silently made her way through the small garden leading to Mark Adam's studio. She knew, after the fire, her time was going to be limited if Moss had anything to do with it. She also knew that, Moss or not, she wasn't going to give up her investigation, which meant she had to make the most of the time left to her.

Pulling out her penlight, she examined the lock on the

front door. Discovering it was pick-proof—Moss's doing, she was sure—she thought wistfully of the key she'd briefly held in her possession. She walked around the side of the building to try the windows. Also locked. Undaunted, she worked her way to the back of the studio. At first glance, the rose trellis didn't look stable enough to be climbed, and under ordinary circumstances Kat never would have attempted it. But these were no ordinary circumstances. She was going to get to the bottom of the problems at Mark's studio, she reflected grimly, if she had to break an arm, leg, or neck trying.

Tugging off her rain poncho, Kat pocketed her tiny flashlight and grabbed on to the trellis. Ignoring the ominous creaking, she placed her sneakered foot on the first lattice bar and tentatively put her weight on it. It promptly snapped in two. Kat bit her lip. Stretching, she put her foot on the second piece of lathing and very, very slowly pulled herself up. It held. Letting out her breath, Kat tried the next slat. It creaked but held.

Privately acknowledging that if she weighed five pounds more she would probably be sprawled on the ground, she carefully made her way up to the roof, checking periodically to make sure no one was watching. She paused to catch her breath when she reached the top, then tested the drain gutter. It passed inspection, so she braced her feet against it and hoisted herself up . . . and managed to dislodge one of the roof tiles. It skittered past her leg and fell with a noisy clatter onto the sidewalk. Kat stopped breathing. Spread-eagled, she clung to the remaining rain-slicked tiles. Two minutes passed. Three minutes. Kat inhaled and lifted her head.

She already knew the skylight over her desk was stuck shut. The one over the studio, however, was not. Flattened against the rough tiles, Kat edged her way toward it. A quick examination certified that, with a little effort, it was possible to lift the skylight open from the outside. Kat succeeded on the third try.

Clinging by her fingertips, she boosted herself up and

dropped herself to the studio, nearly spearing herself on a pink-and-orange umbrella. How Mark could keep his person so neat and tidy and have a studio that looked like a cyclone had hit it was beyond her. Shaking her head, Kat clicked on her penlight and stepped around the two tubs of sand Mark had had delivered the previous afternoon for a "beach" shoot Monday. Then she stopped. As she stared, a grain of sand moved. Then another. Bending down, Kat aimed the narrow beam of light directly on the sand. Two more grains jumped. The sand was infested with fleas.

Mark, bless him, seemed to be prepared for any and all eventualities, however, including marauding insects. Suspecting these had arrived courtesy of Mark's saboteur, Kat located a can of Raid and gave the entire area a thorough dousing. Making a mental note to have the offending tubs replaced before Monday's shoot, she returned to her search. Two minutes later she found the evidence she was seeking. Matching up Mark's logbook with the props to be used the next day, she unearthed two other instances of even more obvious sabotage. Someone was systematically booby-trapping all the props, and they were doing it ahead of time. So much for coincidence.

Walking across the dew-dampened grass of Golden Gate Park, Kat drew in a deep breath of cool sea air. She knew it for certain now. The ladder had definitely been tampered with; the coffeepot probably had, too; her swivel chair had unswiveled right out from under her one day after the darkroom fire; and someone had loosened the same ceiling tile that had nearly beaned one of her predecessors. Unless she was developing a strong streak of paranoia, someone besides Moss was evidently trying to "encourage" her to leave Mark's employment. That, however was no need for panic.

What *was* cause for panic, was Moss himself.

No doubt about it, after that near-kiss, a night of insomnia, and a distinct lack of excitement at the thought of scooping him on the case, she was definitely falling for him—and not just from ladders. Moss Adams. She shook her head in self-disgust. The man who was doing his best to torpedo her career, for heaven's sake. How could she possibly be attracted to him? She had to be losing her mind, obviously. Why else would she even consider entering into a relationship with a man who was not only her adversary professionally—they were working on the same case, after all—but precisely the kind of man she'd sworn to avoid? Nothing threatened a man like an independent woman, especially the sort of man who assumed that all females needed protecting. How was Moss going to feel when he realized that she was not only more liberated than he thought, but that she was infinitely capable of defending herself as well, if not better, than he was? He was going to feel exactly as Derek had: emasculated. And his apparent interest in her would dry up like raisins under the summer sun.

Unless she was a masochist and wanted to be rejected by a man for a second time in her life, she knew she had two choices: She could either try not to get involved with Moss, or she could try to keep him from finding out who and what she was.

Or she could try, however futilely, to do both.

A flock of sea gulls circled noisily overhead. Weaving her way in and out of a shady dell of pink and white rhododendrons, Kat slipped off her heavy oyster-white cardigan. She was halfway across the sunny meadow and had just passed a policewoman patrolling the park on horseback when she felt the nape of her neck begin to warm.

Kat stopped short. The distinctive feeling had nothing whatsoever to do with the sun overhead. It was a sixth sense she'd developed over the past few years, and it invariably meant only one thing: She was being followed.

Spinning around, Kat saw him standing in the concealing shade of a large eucalyptus tree, and from the windblown condition of his sun-gold hair and the fog-dampened look of the brown tweed blazer topping his jeans, he had been following her for some time.

Knowing he'd been spotted, Moss gave her an engaging smile. Kat didn't smile back. Instead, turning abruptly, she started to walk briskly away from him across the wide expanse of lawn. Out of the corner of her eye, she saw Moss following her. Determined to elude him, she picked up speed. She was sprinting down a winding path she thought would take her farther away from her pursuer when she ran headlong into him. Strong, wool-clad arms halted her in midstride.

Catching her breath, Kat pushed away from his protective embrace and gave him a rebellious look. "Will you please stop following me!"

"Stop running away," Moss suggested, "and I won't have to."

He looked barely out of breath, Kat noticed irritably, while she was wheezing for air like a beached whale. Clearly assuming she was in no condition to protest, Moss slipped a muscled arm through hers and started to lead her forward. "You really ought to get more exercise," he advised solemnly as she continued to struggle to fill her lungs. "It's bad for the heart when you—"

"Look." Stopping abruptly, Kat extricated her arm from his and faced him squarely. "I don't know why you've been following me, but you might as well know I came here to relax, and I have no intention of letting you spoil such a perfectly lovely day for me. I absolutely, positively don't want to fight with you."

"Good." His smile broadened. "I absolutely, positively don't want to fight with you either." Again he extended his bent arm. "Pax?"

Kat pointedly ignored it. Placing her hands on her hips, she considered him with patent distrust. "Don't give me that innocent look. I'm not buying it."

"You're mad at me?"

"Mad? Mad?" Kat snorted in disbelief. "Of course I'm not mad. I'm furious."

"Why?"

Kat threw her hands up in despair at the question. "Why do you think? You told Mark about the fire." She eyed him accusingly, daring him to deny it.

He didn't. The tawny eyebrows merely rose in mild surprise. "Of course I told him. I told you I would. Wouldn't you have done the same thing in my place?"

"Yes, but that doesn't make me any less annoyed at you."

"Mark didn't fire you," he pointed out.

"That doesn't make me any less angry at you, either."

Moss shook his gilded head and sighed in amusement. "That's what I like about you, shortstuff. You're always so reasonable. Come have lunch with me. It's too nice a day not to share it with someone."

As Kat opened her lips to deliver her own opinion on that subject, he deftly clamped his hand over her mouth. "You've got to eat," he said reasonably. "Why not with me?"

Her pithy retort muffled, Kat pried his warm, faintly rough hand from her mouth, finger by finger, and smiled sweetly up at him. "How many reasons would you like? One dozen? Two?"

Clucking his tongue lightly, Moss chided, "And you were the one who said you didn't want to fight."

Draping an arm across her shoulders, he guided her to the middle of the sun-drenched meadow. "This looks like a good spot." He surveyed the Eden-like surroundings with pleasure. "What do you think?"

"You wouldn't want to know what I think," Kat assured him.

Casually removing his arm from her shoulders, Moss placed the wicker picnic hamper he'd been holding at his feet, opened it, and pulled out a tartan plaid stadium blanket. Dropping himself gracefully into a cross-legged position, he caught Kat's hand and tugged lightly until she, too, was sitting on the woolly ground cover.

Opening the basket, Moss peered inside. "Let's see," he mused, "what shall we start with? Ah yes, the wine."

Watching as he brought out a bottle of California Pinot Chardonnay, Kat wondered why she wasn't able to stay mad at him for more than two minutes at a time.

"You do this often, do you?" she asked.

Moss glanced up. "Do what?"

"Kidnap women in the park and force them to have lunch with you."

"Not often." Smiling at her unmollified expression, he neatly uncorked the bottle, reached once again into the picnic hamper, and handed Kat two wineglasses. "Would you mind holding these while I pour?"

Filling each glass half-full of the pale, straw-colored wine, he recorked the bottle and rested it against the basket. Then, balancing his glass between his folded legs, he reached once again into the hamper's depths and brought out a creamy white chunk of Monterey Jack cheese. Slicing off a generous portion, he placed it on one of the square whole-wheat crackers, also extracted from the hamper, and handed it to her.

Thinking that cheese and crackers was probably the extent of Moss's culinary talents, Kat ate half a dozen before she realized it was only an appetizer. She watched in amazement as Moss dug deeper into the wicker hamper and produced a deliciously browned, delectably fragrant broccoli quiche.

Unwrapping it, he glanced up and caught Kat's expression. "And here you thought real men didn't eat quiche," he chided, bringing out a knife and deftly cutting it into wedge-shaped slices.

The last thing she needed, Kat decided, accepting the piece he handed her, was Moss reminding her he was a man! Even if she believed that real men didn't eat quiche—which she didn't—there was no doubt in her mind that the long-limbed creature indolently sitting beside her in the warm spring sun was all man.

Forking off a bite of the broccoli, herb, and cheese pie, Kat tasted it and sighed. "This is incredibly decadent." She took another sip of the tart wine. "I don't think I've ever tasted anything so delicious."

"Thank you."

The way he said it almost made Kat drop her glass. "Don't tell me you made the wine?" She leaned over, trying to see the label.

"No," said Moss idly, "just the quiche."

"Good grief." Kat stared at him, not at all sure how she felt about falling for a man who obviously cooked better than she did.

"Another piece?"

Kat shook her head. "It's wonderful, but I'd better not."

Moss cut himself another sizable slice. "Not on a diet, are you?"

"No," Kat admitted. "I just like to keep things under control."

"I'll bet you do." Moss smiled broadly. "You'd like to keep me under control, wouldn't you?"

Kat didn't know how to answer that. "Are you out of control?"

"I could be, around you, pretty lady," he murmured. "Very easily." He contemplated her slightly flushed face for a moment, then took another bite of quiche. "I like that outfit you have on. Very sexy."

Kat's eyes dropped to her terra-cotta corduroy jumpsuit and back up to Moss. "Thank you. Is that why you're looking at me like I'm the next thing on the menu?"

His mouth curved. "Actually, I'm trying to figure out just what it is about your office persona that bothers me the most. I think I'm seeing the real you today, but I keep getting the feeling you're incognito at the office."

"Incognito?" Kat managed weakly. He couldn't possibly suspect what she was doing at Mark's. Could he?

Moss ran a lazy finger over her collar, inciting her corpuscles to action. "Those suits of yours. The way you pin your hair back. Somehow it doesn't seem like your style. It's almost as if you're in disguise."

Kat swallowed with difficulty. "That's silly."

"Is it?" Moss's gray eyes rested on her free-flowing coppery tresses. "There's no reason, other than the obvious one, you shouldn't be working for Mark, is there?"

Kat suddenly couldn't breathe. "What's the obvious reason?"

"You know that as well as I do. Your continued good health." He picked up the wine bottle and reached out to help steady her hand. "Is there a particular reason you get so jumpy when I'm around?"

"Do I look jumpy?" Kat concentrated on holding her hand still.

Moss refilled her glass. "As a matter of fact, yes. Are you afraid of me?"

Kat couldn't tell what prompted the question. Curiosity? Or dismay? "Should I be afraid of you?" she asked, playing it safe.

His shoulders lifted beneath his tweed blazer. "That depends."

"On what?"

"On what it is you're trying to hide from me," he growled softly.

"You're very suspicious!" Kat protested.

"And you, mystery lady, are *very* evasive. Nothing shady in your past you're trying to forget, is there?"

"Just my ex-husband," Kat lied with false cheer. "Does he count?"

"Not with me. You could have ten exes for all I care. I'd just consider all ten of them dunces for letting a woman like you go."

Wishing she could believe that, Kat looked at him a moment. "This isn't charm surfacing all of a sudden, is it?"

The suspicious note in her voice seemed to amuse him. "What's the matter, shortstuff? Didn't you think I had any?"

"Frankly, no. And, just for the record, my name isn't shortstuff. It's Katrina. My friends call me Kat. *You,*" she enunciated clearly, "can call me—"

"Lover?" he supplied hopefully.

Kat ignored him. "—anything but carrot top or red. Try either one of those," she promised, "and I'll seriously consider homicide."

His laugh was low and rich. Still chuckling softly, he reached into the picnic hamper and brought out a succulent cluster of plump green grapes. Breaking the stem in two, he handed her half.

"Kat's an interesting name." He popped a grape into her startled mouth. "Are you anything like your namesake? Do you have claws, Kat?"

If anyone's going to find out, Kat thought, I'm sure it's going to be you. "I know how to defend myself, if that's what you're asking."

"That could be useful in your present job." He ran a finger down her cheek. "You know, just because you take a class in self-defense twice a week doesn't mean you're indestructible."

Kat gasped. "How did you know I have classes in self-defense?" She wasn't about to tell him she taught them. That would involve further explanations, opening a Pandora's box she'd just as soon not get into.

Moss smiled. "I weaseled it out of Mark. Why don't you just apply for a position someplace else so I can stop worrying about you?"

Kat took a deep breath. "I did apply for other jobs before I came to work for Mark," she said, embroidering on her job history as she went along, mentally vowing to keep her mouth shut around her employer in the future. "I was told I wasn't qualified."

"From the way you've been filling up your wastebasket all week, I'd say you weren't overqualified for this one, either."

Laughing at the teasing dig despite herself, Kat protested, "You can hardly expect me to work at optimum efficiency with you breathing down my neck!"

Moss moved fractionally closer. "I'd *like* to breathe down your neck," he purred. "Why don't you come work for me?"

He was close enough now that Kat could smell the very male scent of his body mingling with the fresh, outdoorsy fragrance of grass and wet earth. She swallowed with difficulty. "Do you pay more than Mark?"

"No, but the fringe benefits aren't bad. Are you going to have dinner with me tonight?"

Kat's thick eyelashes dropped, shielding her eyes from the gleam of desire in his. "I think I'd be safer with an untrained lion."

Moss feigned offense. "What kind of man do you think I am?"

"Don't tempt me," Kat warned lightly, trying desperately

to regain control over her rioting emotions.

"Why not? Everything about *you* tempts *me*." She felt him reach out and gently pull a thick strand of her auburn hair through his long fingers. "Your hair is so beautiful in the sunlight. Soft. Silky. In a way, the copper color reminds me of the Irish setter I had as a boy."

Kat's eyes flew wide open. He was kidding, she hoped.

"I hate to tell you this," she said, masking her irritation, "but being compared to a dog isn't something a girl exactly longs to hear."

Moss nodded solemnly, but Kat caught the laughter dancing in his eyes. "I see what you mean. Maybe I'd better try another comparison."

"Maybe you'd better," Kat agreed, longing to kick him.

She watched him tilt his gilded head to one side, pretending to consider his options. The lines around his eyes deepened suddenly, and so did Kat's dread. "I've got it," he beamed. "A slightly used penny." He caught Kat's stony expression and sighed in feigned chagrin. "No good? I don't suppose comparing it to the leaves on the copper beech tree in my grandmother's yard—?"

Kat shook her head. "No. Absolutely not. Maybe you'd better quit while your shins are still undamaged," she suggested.

His eyes glittering, Moss moved suddenly, and before Kat knew it, she was on her back on the grass with Moss balanced on his elbows on top of her. His long, lean body touched hers from waist to shoulder, but most of his considerable weight was on his arms, not on her. Kat still couldn't breathe.

"What are you doing?" she squeaked.

He smiled down at her. "I decided that what I needed was a better look." Bringing a strand of her hair to his lips as Kat watched in mild alarm, he closed his eyes briefly. When he opened them again, Kat's whole body tingled from head to foot.

"What your hair really reminds me of," he said in a deep, husky purr that sent her pulse rate reeling out of control again, "is strawberries and honey, and smoldering embers.

I smell it, and I think of soft summer nights and sweet fragrant wine. And when I touch it," he said even more softly, "I imagine making hot, passionate love with you in the amber glow of a fire with soft music in the background and no one and nothing to bother us."

"Good grief," said Kat faintly.

"And you thought I wasn't a romantic." He kissed her lightly on the nose. "Are you going to have dinner with me tonight?"

Kat pulled air into her lungs with an effort. "What if I say no?"

His smile was wicked and male and as dangerous as an open flame. "Then I'm going to have to hold you here until you change your mind. We'd end up starving together on the grass."

"Oh. Well, in that case," said Kat breathlessly, "the answer is yes."

Hardly disguising his look of triumph, Moss removed his weight and took her hand to help her up. "Where's your car?"

Standing, Kat pushed her hair back with slightly shaky hands. "In the garage being fixed. I'm on foot." She could still feel the imprint of Moss's hard body on hers, the very masculine musculature molding itself to her softer frame. "I was heading downtown when you accosted me."

Moss fed her the last grape and smiled wryly. "If you can stand riding in a slightly banged-up Corvette, I'll drive you there."

They weren't quite out of the park when the accident happened. Moss had just braked to avoid hitting a pair of children scampering across the road. Two-and-a-half seconds later, a resounding crunch jarred the low-slung car. Metal and fiberglass groaned, glass shattered, and Moss looked into his rearview mirror in total disbelief at the blue Ford parked on his rear bumper.

Sighing in disgust, he opened his door. "I'll be right back."

As Moss climbed out of the car, Kat, too, got out to

survey the damage. She stared apprehensively at the large man approaching them.

"I didn't hit you hard enough to do all that," the giant from the blue car snarled belligerently, pointing at the Corvette.

"No," she heard Moss agree. "Some of it's from the last time I got hit. I haven't had a chance to get to a garage yet. Do you see a tow bar here?"

The rest of the conversation was lost to Kat as she restrained the urge to laugh out loud. Those had been Moss's *exact* words the day she'd hit his car, and he was using them now with a man almost as big as he was. She'd thought he'd been patronizing her then. He hadn't. He'd been reacting, as he was now, like a man understandably irritated by the repeated damage done to his car.

Kat contemplated him with new eyes and shook her head in wonderment. She'd obviously misjudged Moss from the very beginning, and if the interlude in the park hadn't convinced her, this had.

How wrong could a woman be about a man?

Kat was humming happily, obliviously off-key, when her brother appeared at her bedroom door, sandwich in hand. "You need help?"

Too pleased with the day's events to mind Ken's latest raid on her refrigerator, Kat abandoned her stuck zipper. "If you're offering, I'm accepting."

Laying down his sandwich, Ken turned her around to the light. Kat felt the zipper go up. "I always knew brothers were good for something," she murmured, sitting in front of her mirror.

Ken leaned against her dresser and retrieved his sandwich. "You're in a good mood," he said, taking a large bite.

"I've had a very prosperous day," Kat confided, applying a second coat of brown mascara to her already darkened lashes.

"Your investigation at Mark Adams's studio is progressing?"

"Among other things." Kat flicked a comb through her hair. She'd felt saucy and happy and definitely on top of the world all afternoon. And not just because of Moss, she admitted.

After he'd dropped her off downtown, she'd caught a cable car to Chinatown, checking to make certain she wasn't being followed, then practically danced the rest of the way to Emma Li's apartment for their prearranged meeting...

"It was a jade ring." Emma Li's exotic dark eyes assessed Kat as she poured two cups of tea. "Very large and very valuable."

Kat took the proffered cup. "Any idea what happened to it?"

The other woman absently touched the red silk of her Mandarin collar and shrugged. "Who knows? The lights were out, and at least eight other people were running around like headless chickens when that stupid tear gas was let loose. All I know is that you can forget trying to locate it at Mark's studio. It's nice of you to offer to look for it, but Mark and I practically upended the building searching for it. Which means, since it figured prominently in the layout, that Mark will either have to scrap the film he's taken or come up with a matching ring."

"Mark's rescheduled the shoot for you, then?" Kat had asked, her mind busily digesting this latest bit of information.

Emma Li flipped back her long black hair over her shoulders. "He's trying to, but Frank Morgan tells me where to go and when, and he's balking. And frankly, as much as I like Mark, it wouldn't exactly desolate me to have the job given to someone else..."

Kat smiled into the dresser mirror. Not a bad day, all in all, she decided in satisfaction. She'd finally made what looked like a breakthrough in the case, and tonight, if all went well, she might make a breakthrough with Moss as well.

She looked up at Ken. "Can I borrow your brains for a minute?"

He grunted. "That depends on what you plan to do with them."

"Nothing dastardly. I want to know what you'd do if the things that are happening at Mark Adams's studio were happening to you."

"I don't have the imagination you do. Give me a scenario."

Kat thought a minute. "Okay. You're doing the cover for a book about Cleopatra and Mark Antony. Your model dresses in Egyptian garb and is about to put on her Cleo wig when she finds someone has snipped it into five pieces. What do you do?"

"Get another wig. Is this the sort of thing that's been happening?"

"You wouldn't believe what's been happening. Okay, let's try again. Forget the wig. Your model is in the process of putting on her makeup and discovers, too late, that someone has swapped Superglue for her fake eyelash adhesive. She freaks out. What do you do?"

Ken watched Kat apply lip gloss. "Calm her down."

"What if you couldn't?"

"Well, Madam Prosecutor, I'd reschedule the sitting."

Kat nodded. So far, so good. "What if she couldn't come back? This isn't the first time something strange has happened to her at your studio, and her modeling agency refuses to let her return. What do you do?"

Ken shrugged. "I'd get someone else."

Kat tried to contain her excitement. "Can you do that? I thought the client picked the model. That they worked directly with the modeling agency, and if you lost the model you lost the account."

"Not always. About half the time I choose the model."

That's what she'd wanted to know. Assuming the shoots were scrapped when trouble arose, Kat had concluded the sabotage was regularly losing Mark business when, in fact, at least in some cases it was nothing more than an inconvenience. Which meant that, whatever the motive was, bankrupting *Mark* apparently wasn't it.

Ken caught Kat's expression. "Did I help?"

"I'm not sure yet," Kat said, feeling closer to solving the puzzle than ever before, "but yes, I think you may have. Want to hear something interesting? I don't think all this sabotage is aimed at putting Mark Adams out of business at all. If that were the case, they wouldn't keep doing things like starting these little fires, would they? They'd just burn the place down. There must be another motive."

Ken stopped chewing. "Fires? What fires?"

"Never mind," Kat lilted. Smiling in satisfaction, she clipped on a pair of gold hoop earrings.

Looking resigned, Ken picked up a bottle of cologne from her dresser and held it beneath his nose. After a moment, he eyed Kat's elegant copper-and-gold silk evening pajamas as though noticing them for the first time. "You're certainly all dolled up," he noted with brotherly interest. "Hot date?"

Kat winked at him in the mirror. "One can only hope." She smudged a last-minute application of gold eyeshadow over her lids.

"This sounds serious. Maybe I should go along and chaperon."

Kat gave her brother a sunny smile. "Over my dead body."

Ken shook his head. "Definitely serious. Anyone I know?"

Kat took a step back and surveyed herself critically in the mirror. "I don't think so. I only met him this week." She turned around. "How do I look?"

"Devastating," her sibling confirmed. "You'll knock his socks off."

"It's not his socks I'm interested in," Kat murmured with a flirty smile.

Ken stepped back as she sprayed herself with her favorite cologne. "By the way, while I think of it, I had an interesting visitor this morning. Do you know anyone named Moss?

CHAPTER
Seven

KAT WENT MOTIONLESS. Certain her ears were deceiving her, she turned slowly and stared at her brother. "Moss?" she repeated rustily.

"Yeah. Big guy. Blond. Well-built. He stopped by the studio today, and I wondered—"

"When?"

Looking vaguely taken aback by the terse question, Ken shrugged. "I don't know. Five or ten minutes after you left."

Five or ten minutes after he'd followed her to her brother's studio, she surmised, and then she saw her head off on foot toward the park.

"Damn!" Kat slammed the cologne bottle down on the dresser, rattling the row of cosmetics. "Damn, damn, damn."

"I guess that means you know him," Ken said with a wary smile. "I wondered. He acted as if he knew you pretty well."

He did, did he? "What did he want?" As if she didn't know! The sneaking, low-down, conniving—

"Nothing much. He looked at a few paintings—"

"Did he ask you anything about me?"

"Well, not exactly."

Kat's eyes narrowed ominously. "What does 'not exactly' mean, exactly?"

Ken shifted position, looking distinctly uncomfortable. "What are you getting so upset about?"

"Upset? I'm not upset. What did he say?"

Ken scratched his nose. "Well, he wanted to know if you were still working for that insurance company in L.A.—"

"Johnson and Beckman," Kat supplied, feeling faintly ill.

"Yeah." Ken nodded. "That was it."

"And you told him—?"

"That, to my knowledge, you'd never lived in Los Angeles. That the only time you haven't lived in the city was when you and Derek were married and—what's the matter now?"

"Damn!"

Ken's mouth twisted. "You've already said that. You're not usually this inarticulate. Is there some problem? Where you live isn't a secret, is it?"

"He's investigating me!" Kat wailed in anger and dismay. "He's checking up on the résumé I gave Mark Adams!"

"Are you sure?"

"Sure? Of course I'm sure!" Kat sat heavily on the edge of her bed. "I wish to heaven I weren't," she added bitterly as her eyes fell to her strappy high-heeled sandals. She'd been looking forward to this evening so much, and now . . . now she wasn't sure she could even look at Moss without wanting to do him physical injury.

"Why would he be checking out your résumé?" Ken looked disturbed but still confused.

"Because he's Mark's brother, that's why. And because he's a private investigator."

"Oh."

"Oh, indeed."

"I think I'm sorry I said anything. But honestly, Kat, he didn't seem like the type to do anything, well, underhanded." He stopped at Kat's unladylike snort. "No, really. I got the feeling he was asking about you because, well, because he cared about you."

She'd thought he cared, too, Kat reflected, filled with acute self-loathing. More fool her. He'd probably asked her out tonight simply to complete his investigation. What was he planning? A little wining and dining? Getting her off guard before he lowered the boom? He obviously thought he had her where he wanted her.

Well, he could think again.

The trick to keeping a cool head tonight, Kat decided bleakly, was to keep thinking about Derek all evening, remembering everything that had gone wrong with their relationship and reminding herself that Moss was basically a sneaky, albeit attractive, creature, not to be trusted. She was going to keep her composure, keep in control of the situation, and keep him at arm's length the entire evening if she had to place a chair between them to accomplish the feat.

Easier said than done.

Moss picked her up promptly at eight o'clock, and even as he helped her into the damaged Corvette Kat recognized she was going to have her work cut out for her. Not only did Moss look impossibly handsome in the oatmeal-colored suit, crisp tan shirt, and brown tie, but her own body had somehow gotten its loyalties mixed up and was firmly on his side. Kat shivered as his hot gray eyes skimmed appreciatively over her slim figure, taking in the artfully draped neckline of her softly shimmering outfit. It was calculated to tantalize, giving the barest glimpses of the skin beneath. And Moss was looking properly tantalized and hungry to see more.

"Very, very nice," he murmured with purely masculine pleasure underscoring his faintly gravelly voice. His hand brushed against her full sleeve as he reached to insert the key into the car's ignition.

With a quick intake of breath, Kat deliberately moved farther away from him. Even in the dim light, she saw Moss's eyes narrow in speculation. With slow, deliberate movements, he leaned back in his bucket seat and placed his hands on the leather-wrapped steering wheel.

"All right," he said calmly. "Let's get it over with so we can enjoy the rest of the evening. You found out I talked with your brother, and you're angry."

His very calmness enflamed Kat's temper. "Don't I have a right to be angry?" She turned and faced him. "You're treating me like a suspect!"

"As far as I'm concerned, you became a suspect the minute you began working for my brother." He sounded imminently reasonable and thoroughly logical. Which only served to make Kat madder.

"You could have asked me, if there was something specific you wanted to know!"

"I did try," he reminded her with what sounded like restrained exasperation. "You haven't exactly been cooperating."

"So you probe into my past," Kat stormed, "interrogate my family, leave no stone unturned—"

"And a very interesting pastime it's turned out to be, too." Moss picked up her left hand, holding on when she would have jerked it back, and caressed the palm with his thumb. "Imagine Lawrence Hallman's surprise—and mine, too—when it turned out he supposedly employed you for four years but couldn't recall your name."

"I can explain that," Kat said aloofly.

"I wait with bated breath," said Moss quite dryly.

Kat cleared her throat, aware of his scrutiny. "Well, I may have fudged a little on my job history," she conceded.

"You mean you lied." Moss squeezed her hand.

Kat sighed in surrender. "All right. I lied. But I had a good reason," she added in self-defense.

"No doubt. Tell me, was there anything on that résumé of yours that wasn't total fiction?"

My name, Kat thought, giving him a wan smile.

Moss started the car. "That's what I thought."

The restaurant he chose was in the newly renovated section of town near the Embarcadero, just far enough off the beaten track to miss the mainstream of tourists. Silently considering the gilt-haired man seated opposite her, Kat wondered why she was feeling so guilty about getting their evening off on the wrong foot when, in her view, she had every right to be angry with him.

Moss was obviously going to keep prying until he knew everything he wanted to know about her. Why couldn't she just tell him the whole truth and be done with it? Because, a small, irritating inner voice pointed out, you know what's going to happen if you do. She already suspected she was more than half in love with him, but whatever Moss felt for her—and she wasn't sure yet just what it was—she didn't think it would withstand the truth. When Moss discovered to what extent she'd lied to him, he was going to despise her.

Filled with despair, Kat surveyed him across the candlelit table abundantly set with china and silver. "Are you put out with me because I refuse to blab about my personal life or because I refuse to leave Mark's studio?"

Moss laid down the menu he'd been perusing. "I'm not put out, sweetheart. You're the one who can't seem to control your temper."

"Domineering males have a way of enflaming it," Kat shot back.

Moss leaned forward, and his voice dropped to a rough whisper. "Come home with me tonight," he said in the soft purr that made Kat tingle all the way to her toes, "and I'll do my best to enflame the rest of you."

Shocked by her reaction to the warm intimacy he had instantly created between them, Kat licked her dry lips. "I don't want to get involved with you," she whispered back, her voice husky with suppressed emotion.

"No," Moss corrected gently, "you're *afraid* to get involved with me. What I haven't quite figured out yet is why. Are you hiding something from me?"

"Who, me?"

Smiling wryly, Moss shook his head. "You're the only woman I've ever met who didn't want to talk about herself."

Kat gulped. "There's nothing much to tell. My past would bore you."

"Honey," he growled, "lots of words could be applied to you, but *boring* sure as hell isn't one of them. Are you ready to order?"

"Are you sure you still want to feed me?"

"Considering how little you ate at lunch, I consider it my pleasurable duty to make sure you don't go hungry tonight." He picked up the menu again. "Do you like seafood?"

"Do fishes swim?"

"Never having studied marine biology, I'm going to take a stab at that one and conclude your answer is yes. I'm glad. It's excellent here." He smiled with devastating warmth, and the dark cloud that had threatened to settle over their table dissipated, leaving in its wake the black velvet night and the mesmerizing heat in Moss's gray eyes.

With almost tangible electricity sizzling in the air, they zestfully worked their way through parchment-thin slices of salmon with melon, clam bisque, shrimp and cucumber salad, and coquilles Saint Jacques. Pleasant background music, excellent service, and a fragrant Johannesburg Riesling accompanied each delectable bite. They had just finished the pièce de résistance—almond crêpes flambées—and were polishing off the feast with Kahlúa and Colombian coffee, when Moss looked at her over his liqueur glass and said quite gently, "You're still mad as hell at him, aren't you?"

Kat ate the last bite of her crêpe and put down her dessert fork. "Him, who?"

Moss lifted his glass to his lips. "You know who. That ex-husband of yours. What do I do, remind you of him? Is that why you react like a scalded cat whenever I try to get too close to you?"

Perhaps it was the wine or the serene atmosphere, but somehow the question neither startled nor alarmed her. But it did make her pause and think.

She wasn't confusing Moss with Derek, was she? she asked herself in all honesty. Physically they were nothing alike. Derek was brown-eyed and dark-haired and far from athletic. The only thing he'd ever exercised was his brain. But, like Moss, he'd thought he knew what was best for her, and the consequences had been disastrous.

That didn't mean, of course, that she and Moss had no future together, Kat concluded, trying desperately to believe it.

"I'm not discussing my marriage with you," she told him, firmly resolving to put it all behind her.

"I don't know what he did to you, but believe me, you're overcompensating if you think that by pushing me away you can avoid getting hurt again. Living hurts. Sometimes loving hurts. Avoiding involvement with me isn't going to destroy your past; it's just going to jeopardize your future happiness."

"Thank you, Freud."

"Stop being so secretive," Moss scolded. "Talking about your past is supposed to be cathartic."

Kat gave him a sunny smile. "Good, then let's talk about yours. How long were you married?"

The tawny eyebrows lifted. "Two years. How did you know I'd been married?"

Kat wrinkled her nose. "From Mark, of course. How else do you and I find out anything about each other? What was she like?"

Moss considered the question. "Sweet. Feminine. High-strung."

A feeling of inexplicable desolation swept through Kat. "You loved her."

"I wouldn't have married her if I hadn't," said Moss in a reasonable tone. "But it didn't take me very long to figure out that in my profession a nervous, helpless wife was worse than no wife at all. When that happened, the love just sort of withered away into frustration. Something I don't expect is going to be a problem with us. You're sure not helpless—"

"—and you're already frustrated," Kat finished for him, stirring cream into her coffee.

Moss smiled mischievously at her. "It's nothing a cold shower won't remedy. At least temporarily. What about you?"

"I prefer bubble baths myself. Very soothing on the—"

"Kat . . ."

Moss's warning growl stopped her. Wrong answer, she decided. She gave him an innocent look. "You were asking?"

"Did you love what's-his-name?"

"Derek," Kat supplied. "And yes, I did once, before it became obvious we just didn't see eye-to-eye on some very basic issues."

"What was he like?"

Kat toyed with her spoon. "Smooth. Suave. The perfect lawyer."

"A lawyer, huh?"

"Mmm. A very good one, too. He managed to walk out of our marriage with everything worth more than a nickel. Am I sounding a tad bitter?"

"Just a tad." Moss lifted his coffee cup. "How long were you married?"

"Not quite a year." Kat paused, then added reluctantly, "I keep telling myself I ought to be grateful I found out what kind of a man he was before we had children, but the truth is, most of the time I'm just too damned mad at him to be grateful for much of anything." She rested her spoon carefully on her saucer. "Can we talk about something else, now? I hate talking about Derek."

"I'm not crazy about the subject myself," Moss admitted, "but I don't want him looming between us all night like a specter from the past, either."

It was one of those horrible little ironies of life, Kat decided, that the mere mention of his name seemed to conjure Derek up out of thin air. Moss had just paid their dinner check and gone to collect her wrap from the coat check when she saw him walk into the restaurant.

At first she simply refused to believe it was really he with the lovely blonde swathed in white fur, but of course it was. Dark, handsome, and dashing in a black topcoat, he was smiling down at something the blonde had said when, for no apparent reason, his dark eyes rose and caught Kat staring straight at him.

He looked as shocked as she did, Kat thought fleetingly,

but he recovered quickly. Removing his coat to reveal a sleek, continental striped suit beneath, he murmured something to the blonde, who looked up quickly, saw Kat, and nodded. Then, slipping his arm through hers, they began making their way toward Kat.

"Don't tell me," Moss's soft, growly voice murmured in her ear, "let me guess. The infamous Derek."

Kat looked up at him with stricken eyes. "There isn't a trapdoor beneath my feet, by any chance?" She tried to smile and failed miserably.

Moss studied her tight-lipped face, his eyes a very dark gray. "There's no need to be afraid of him. I'm bigger than he is."

At the obviously teasing remark, Kat felt some of the tension leave her wire-taut muscles. "I'm not afraid of him," she said honestly, "but this is going to be very awkward. I haven't seen him in over six months. All the wounds we inflicted on each other should be healed, but somehow just the sight of him makes me want to do something terribly uncivilized."

"You shock me."

"Stop laughing at me," Kat wailed softly. "This is serious! I'm going to end up embarrassing both of us, I just know it. Lord, what's he *doing* here?"

Moss draped her fringed shawl gently across her tense shoulders, his fingers lightly caressing the back of her neck. "Cheer up, tiger." He gave her a slight comforting squeeze. "I'm here if you need me."

Kat would've just as soon disappeared, but it was too late for that.

"Hello, Katrina." Derek's baritone forced her to look up from the floor. "How are you?"

Though his lawyer's smile was firmly in place, Kat could see he was warily awaiting some kind of confrontation. Out of sheer spite, Kat decided to surprise him. She smiled brightly. "Hello, Derek," she said in dulcet tones. "What a pleasure to see you again."

The smile never faltered, but Kat felt the distinct pleasure of having shaken the unflappable Derek. He turned to Moss, his eyes openly speculative. "I don't believe we've met. I'm Derek Langley."

Kat saw something flicker briefly in Moss's gray eyes as he extended his hand. "Moss Adams."

As the two men shook hands, Kat faced the lovely blonde at Derek's side, who in turn was looking at Kat with obvious curiosity. Confident of her ability to carry the whole thing off now that the worst was past, Kat gave the other woman a smile.

"I'm sorry." She held out her hand. "I don't think we've ever met. You must be Jane."

The nightmare was beginning to come true. As soon as she said it, Kat realized with horrible certainty that it *wasn't* Jane, but it was too late to retract the words.

The momentarily surprised expression on the blonde's face changed into a friendly smile as she clasped Kat's hand. "Actually," she said, apparently used to the confusion over her identity, "I'm Sandy Rice."

Without meaning to, Kat found herself looking back at Derek in question.

"I thought you knew," he said. "Jane and I are getting a divorce."

He said it so matter-of-factly, Kat thought, as though it hardly mattered. Kat found herself wondering if Jane, too, had failed to live up to his expectations.

The situation was degenerating fast. Moss was looking infuriatingly relaxed, Kat noted. Feeling justifiably homicidal, she threw him a look that should have fried him on the spot and prayed fervently for the other couple to change the subject. What she got in answer to her prayers, however, wasn't exactly what she'd expected.

Sandy Rice gave Kat an admiring smile. "Derek has told me about your being a private investigator," she piped up, apparently hoping to retrieve the situation and eliminate the sudden awkwardness. "Being a private eye must be terribly exciting."

CHAPTER
Eight

THE HAND DRAPED over Kat's shoulder suddenly seemed as heavy as an iron manacle.

"It certainly has its moments," she said weakly to Sandy. And this was definitely not one of them!

Kat found it impossible to look up at Moss. How was he taking the news? Was he going to give away the fact that he hadn't known she was a private eye? Or would he play along and settle with her later? Lord, how did she get herself into these messes?

"It's a very unusual profession for a woman," Sandy burbled on enthusiastically.

"Katrina has always been something of a trendsetter," Derek remarked dryly. "It's a challenge just to keep up with her. Wouldn't you agree, Moss?" He turned to Kat's companion.

Kat felt Moss's warm fingers tighten almost imperceptibly on her shoulder. "I would indeed." He spoke with silky menace that even Kat could hear. "Then again, what real man could ever resist a challenge?"

79

Derek visibly retreated, and even though Kat told herself Moss probably wasn't defending her so much as putting Derek in his place, it was all she could do not to jump up and hug him.

"Yes, well." Though smiling, Kat's former husband was obviously anxious to avoid a confrontation with Moss. "If you'll excuse us, I believe our table is ready."

Kat watched Derek execute a swift exit with his date, then peeked cautiously at Moss, trying to decipher his mood as he guided her out of the restaurant.

Rain descended in sheets from heavily overcast skies. Glancing up briefly, Moss dug out his car keys. "You'll ruin your outfit if it gets wet. Wait here, and I'll bring the car around."

Kat touched his sleeve as he turned to leave. "Moss, thank you. I—" His utter lack of expression stopped her.

"Wait here," he repeated, and left.

Huddled under the restaurant's canopy, Kat hugged her thin shawl around her and watched him disappear into the wet, black night. Even if it hadn't been raining buckets, she suspected, he still would have offered to get the car. He obviously needed a moment away from her. Time to think. Time to reconsider. Time to figure out how to tactfully end their date at 9:30?

Everything had changed with a few carelessly spoken words, and it was her fault, not Sandy's. How could she have been stupid enough not to realize Moss would find out sooner or later what her profession really was? And that it would be far better coming from her than by accident as it had tonight?

Kat sighed in despair. The evening had definitely become an unqualified disaster. It didn't seem possible that things could go from bad to worse, but of course they did.

Deeply mired in her thoughts, Kat didn't hear or see the young man running toward her until he was almost upon her. At the sound of the Corvette's powerful engine, she looked up just in time. The man's arm had already arced out, reaching for the sequined purse dangling from her fingers by its thin gold chain.

There wasn't time to think, only to react, and because of Kat's rigorous training in self-defense, that's exactly what she did. Dropping her purse to the wet sidewalk, she turned, and with a smooth, swift lift of her leg and an automatic "Hah!" she kicked the charging man squarely in the kneecap.

As she straightened her silky tunic, smoothed her hair back into place, and tried in general to look as though dispatching would-be robbers was something she did in the normal course of the day, Kat decided it was hard to tell who was more surprised: the stunned-looking young man scrambling to his feet and limping hurriedly away; or Moss, who was staring at her through the Corvette's windshield as though he'd never really seen her before. As perhaps, Kat realized, he hadn't.

Stopping the car at the curb, Moss climbed out and came toward her slowly. His thoughtful gray eyes flicked briefly to the retreating back of her assailant and then to her action-flushed face. "You okay?"

"Yes." Kat nodded, feeling uncomfortably naked before his steady gaze. "He was going to grab my purse," she explained unnecessarily with a crooked smile.

"More fool him." Without another word, Moss handed her into the low black car and climbed in beside her.

They'd driven almost two blocks before Kat got up the nerve to speak again. "Where are you taking me?"

Hope flared and died as Moss negotiated a turn and said calmly, "Home."

So there it was then, the end of what had begun to look like something special. Filled with self-recrimination, Kat turned toward the side window to hide the sudden brightness in her eyes. She should have forseen this. No, she *had* forseen it, but she'd ignored her better judgment and fallen in love with Moss while trying to delay the inevitable.

She'd been a fool to hide the truth from him. But it wasn't just that she'd lied to him, she suspected; it was *what* she was that was now giving Moss second thoughts. What else had she expected? If nothing threatened a man like an independent woman, then nothing turned one off faster than one in the same occupation. Were all her relationships with men doomed before they'd even begun because of her profession? It was beginning to look that way. It had already broken up one marriage and was well on the way to destroying her blossoming relationship with Moss.

Contemplating the bleak future before her, it was another five minutes before Kat realized Moss was driving in the wrong direction if he planned on taking her back to her apartment.

"I thought you said you were taking me home," she said in confusion as they passed yet another unfamiliar landmark.

"I am." Moss sounded calm but preoccupied. "Mine."

Kat studied his roughly chiseled profile in the dark. "I don't understand. I thought—"

"I know what you thought." The smoke-colored eyes slid her way. "Honey," he added in that soft, dangerous purr that ruffled every one of her nerve endings, "you and I have a lot to talk about. We might as well start tonight. Sit back and relax. We're almost there."

Which meant, Kat supposed, as she sat back anything but relaxed, she was going to have a lot of explaining to do before the final good-bye. Wonderful.

As Moss turned the Corvette onto Laguna Street, Kat sat up with interest. Somehow she'd expected him to live in a thoroughly modern steel-and-concrete high-rise, something clean and efficient, requiring little or no attention. She was wrong. Unpredictable as ever, Moss parked the car in front of a charming dove-gray Victorian with geranium-filled window boxes, generous bay windows, and a columned front porch.

The interior was equally surprising. Moss led her through the foyer into a large living room that was pleasantly masculine but not aggressively so, with a comfortable cocoa-brown corduroy couch settled before the white brick fireplace. Fawn-beige carpeting cushioned her feet, accenting the faint stripes in the off-white draperies hanging at the tall, scroll-worked windows. The polished oak woodwork gleamed richly in the light of a brass chandelier.

Taking off his jacket and hanging it on the antique coat

tree near the door, Moss studied her. "Coffee? Or brandy?"

Reluctantly, Kat met his eyes fully for the first time since Sandy Rice had spilled the beans. "No arsenic?"

His faint smile gave her no clue to his mood. Slipping her shawl from her shoulders, he draped it over the coat tree and held out his hand. "Come into the kitchen with me."

Hesitantly placing her hand in the dry warmth of his, Kat surveyed her surroundings as Moss led her down the long hallway. Unlike most older homes, this one, though obviously built in the latter part of the last century, had none of the cramped darkness of so many of its peers. After a moment Kat realized why. Someone had painstakingly renovated the house, taking out walls to open up the interior while maintaining its original elegance. What had probably once been a separate formal dining room was now connected smoothly to the kitchen to form a pleasant family room. The off-white walls helped to brighten what had probably been a lightless room, making it a comfortable haven.

That was how she'd describe the house in general, Kat decided. Comfortable and welcoming. Standing next to Moss in the almond-and-brown kitchen, she wondered if it would ever truly welcome her.

Moss opened a fresh can of ground coffee, and the pungent fragrance filled the kitchen as he set to work filling the automatic brewer with water.

"Aren't you going to say anything?" Kat finally asked, leaning against the tiled counter.

"What do you want me to say?" Moss scooped coffee into the paper filter and plugged in the pot.

"Anything," said Kat fervently. "You haven't said more than two words to me since you found out I'm not really a secretary. Couldn't you yell a little? Call me names? Throw something? I know how angry you must be at me for not telling you before."

Something—Kat wasn't sure what—flickered in his dark gray eyes as Moss set to work unknotting his tie. "I'm not angry at you."

No? Well then, why was he looking at her like that? And why was he taking off his tie, if not to strangle her with it?

"You don't believe me, do you?"

Kat wasn't sure what she believed. Or what she wanted. Reassurance, she suspected. "You could try sounding more convincing."

Moss smiled, obviously recognizing the laconic words he'd used on her the first time they'd met. "I could," he agreed, a sudden, dangerous gleam in his silver eyes as he slipped the tie from around his collar. "But since I'm a man of action and not words . . ."

He was incredibly quick for a man of his size, Kat thought fleetingly. Before she could blink, let alone react, he'd looped the length of silk around the nape of her neck and tugged, bringing her gently, inexorably toward him.

Her automatic protest never got past her lips. His firm, warm mouth came down swiftly on hers, claiming possession with a gentle thoroughness that left her dazed and breathless, incapable of anything approaching coherent thought. Rooted to the floor, Kat felt him pull her closer, then still closer, until her trembling body met his.

Ever since she'd met Moss, she'd wondered what would happen if he finally kissed her. Now she knew. Lightning sizzled through her limbs, spreading heat throughout her body. Thunder reverberated after it. The earth moved. Or was that one of San Francisco's famous earthquakes? No, it was definitely Moss. Swaying bonelessly against him, Kat clung to the front of his shirt and felt the muscles of his chest contract. Caught in a maelstrom of emotion, she lifted her face. A trail of kisses rained down over her eyelids, across her cheeks, over her mouth, lingering at the corners before descending with aching slowness down her pulsing throat. Her blood roared through her veins like flood waters bursting over a dam as, with unerring accuracy, he found that traitorous spot behind her ear and proceeded to explore it.

"Moss!" At first Kat's soft gasp went unheeded as his tongue encircled her lobe. Then, with one last lingering foray that threatened to scorch her down to her toes, Moss eased away.

Reluctantly, Kat lifted her lashes and found herself staring into his molten-metal eyes.

"Convinced?" The husky query sent a hot wave of silver shimmering through her veins.

"You're very persuasive," Kat managed shakily.

"I can be even more convincing."

Alarmed, Kat half expected him to demonstrate right then and there, but instead he dropped a chaste kiss on her nose.

Was it over, then? Dammit, she was just beginning to warm up!

Confused, Kat tried to remember the act of breathing as he reached easily into an overhead cabinet and brought down two ceramic mugs. For a long time she was sure he wasn't going to speak. Then, very calmly, he asked, "Why did you keep his name?"

It was the last thing she expected him to say. "What?"

"Langley's name," he clarified. "You're one very independent lady. I wouldn't have expected you to keep his name after the divorce. Why did you?"

Wishing her own brain were functioning as clearly as his apparently was, Kat rubbed her nose, chagrined. This wasn't going to be her favorite confession, she admitted, but Moss deserved an explanation. The only trouble was, if he didn't already have a low opinion of her morals, he soon would.

She hesitated, and when Moss continued to wait for her answer, she sighed. "I did it for revenge," she confessed, her eyes sweeping the maplewood kitchen floor. "I wanted to embarrass him. He hated my being a private investigator. He'd rather be shot than have me use his name on my agency, so I thought I'd keep it just long enough to make him nervous, then go back to my maiden name." She looked up. "You must think I'm awful."

Moss shrugged. "Revenge is a pretty basic emotion. I'd worry about you if you were able to leave your marriage not feeling anything. What's your maiden name?"

"I gather from that question," said Kat very dryly, "that you couldn t read Ken's signature on any of his paintings, either. It's Sinclair."

"*Sin* being the operative word?" Moss sounded vaguely amused.

Kat bit her lip. "I realize it doesn't seem very evident at the moment, but I'm really a very moral, honest person. I don't usually lie so much," she added in dubious self-defense.

"I believe you." Moss handed her a steaming mug of coffee. As Kat took it from him, she caught the gleam in his eyes. He was laughing at her.

"That's awfully decent of you."

"Please." Moss lifted a hand in mock horror. "Call me anything, but don't call me decent. We private eyes have our reputations to think of, you know." As Kat glared at him over the rim of her cup, his smile softened. "Honey," he soothed, "compared to what I did when I first started out, you look like an angel, lies and all. How long have you been an investigator?"

He'd slipped right into the subject without so much as batting an eyelash, Kat reflected. "About a year," she said, wondering if he'd make the connection between the timing of her divorce and the initiation of her career.

"Are you any good at it?"

"Yes. Are you?"

His roguish smile made her cheeks go warm. "I like to think I have some expertise in a number of areas."

Then why hadn't he been able to crack this case? It had been bothering Kat on and off since she'd first found out he was a professional investigator. She didn't doubt his ability. One look at Moss told you he was as competent as they came. So what on earth was the problem?

"Go ahead and ask as long as we're on the subject," he urged, obviously reading her mind. "Why am I taking so long to figure out what's going on at Mark's studio?"

Kat flushed under his steady gaze. "Well, why are you? It's fairly obvious it's sabotage."

"Is it?" He blew into his cup.

"Unless you believe in coincidence, yes. It's also pretty

obvious that Mark's not the real target."

"Is it?"

Kat bit her lip. If he said "Is it?" that way one more time, she was fairly certain she was going to whap him over the head with whatever was available. That she could want Moss *and* want to murder him all at the same time didn't seem the least bit contradictory, considering the man in question.

"You know as well as I do that if someone really wanted to put Mark out of business, they'd think of something more damaging to do than start fires in wastebaskets," Kat said, striving for a calm, reasonable tone when she felt anything but calm or reasonable.

"I see." Moss nodded thoughtfully. "So you think it's his secretaries who are the real targets?"

Somewhere along the line, between worrying about whether or not Moss was going to catch on to what she was doing at the studio and worrying about her growing attraction to him, she'd forgotten about the sabotage involving Mark's secretaries. "Well, no. I—"

"Ah. You think the models are the targets, then."

"Well, yes. As a matter of fact I—"

"If that's the case, then how do you explain what's happened to his secretaries?"

"Well—"

"No doubt you've decided it's connected to the fact that Mark's dated all of them at one time or another."

Kat hadn't realized Mark had been involved with any of his secretaries, let alone all of them. "Well, actually—"

"I suppose you've concluded the same thing about the models who've had trouble there."

Kat hadn't known he'd dated any of his models, either. Remembering an earlier conversation she'd had with her interrogator, Kat accused, "I thought you said Mark never mixed business and pleasure!"

"I said not for long. Let's assume, just for the heck of it, that Mark *is* the target. Who would you say was an obvious suspect?"

Kat's chin came up as she warmed to the subject. "Normally, in an obvious case of repeated sabotage, the culprit is usually a disgruntled ex-employee or a dissastisfied customer. In this case—"

"—considering some of Mark's equipment seems to have been stolen, it might be a supplier who'd like to sell Mark the same camera apparatus twice," Moss added, blandly, "or a competing photographer who thinks Mark's being just a little bit too successful, or someone who thought the site of his studio should've been a park, or just a crackpot who, for some reason which may or may not make any sense at all, has it in for Mark, his secretaries, or even, perhaps, one of the fifty-odd models he uses regularly. Have I covered everything?" he asked of the ceiling in a way that made Kat want to crown him. No one had told her any equipment had disappeared.

"All right." She could feel her face growing hot. "I'm getting the point. Why don't you just call me stupid and be done with it?"

"You're not stupid." Moss held up the coffeepot and put it down again as Kat refused a refill. "You just haven't had your sole attention on this case the way I have for the past two weeks. Not everything is as it first seems," he added. "You, of all people, should know that."

Kat wasn't sure if he was referring to himself or her or both of them.

He finished his coffee, took away her empty mug, and rinsed both under the faucet as Kat watched. It was amazing how easily he seemed to do the most homey of tasks, without looking even remotely domesticated.

"How many steps were there coming into the house?" he asked without warning.

Kat frowned, trying to follow his train of thought. "Six."

Moss smiled back. "Good girl. You're observant. That's a necessary commodity in this profession."

Kat eyed him stonily. "Are you patronizing me?"

"No, just checking out your powers of observation."

"I got your number the first time I met you," she assured him.

For some reason that seemed to amuse him. "Did you indeed? What kinds of jobs have you done in the past?"

Watching him dry his hands, Kat wryly listed her meager string of accomplishments and watched in surprise as his angular face registered genuine sympathy.

"I know how it is in the beginning. It must be especially hard to get established when you're a woman."

"It is," Kat agreed, not sure she trusted the apparent empathy. "I have to be twice as good as a male counterpart, and then I'm still not taken seriously. That's why I took this job: to prove I'm as capable as the next person. Moss," she asked almost in desperation, "aren't you angry with me even a little?"

"You mean for lying to get yourself hired?" He shrugged, stretching the fabric of his shirt over his broad shoulders. "Not particularly. We all do what we have to do to get things done. Knowing why you're so insistent about working for Mark puts some pieces of the puzzle together. And it automatically eliminates you as a suspect. At least now I know why you've been as evasive as hell." He reached out and gently tugged a lock of her hair.

"You're making me feel incredibly guilty." Kat's heart restarted its erratic pounding at the casually affectionate gesture. "Stop being so nice. I'd feel better if you yelled."

"I'm not the yelling type. I save my energy for more meaningful pursuits." His eyes locked onto hers, and Kat's heart skipped three whole beats before it stumbled on.

"Would you be interested in seeing the rest of the house?" Moss asked, his voice low and masculine and very, very enticing.

"I'd love to. As long as you don't get any cute ideas when we come to your bedroom. In fact, let's leave out the upstairs altogether."

"I hate to disappoint you, but my bedroom's on this floor."

"Oh?"

Moss led out an exaggerated sigh as he put his hand under her elbow and led her back down the hallway. "I've never met such a suspicious woman," he complained. "Of course," he added after a thoughtful pause, "I've never met one of my own kind before, either. It's an enlightening experience, to say the least."

Reaching out, he smoothly slid back a decorative panel to reveal a hidden staircase. "Come into my parlor, Katrina Langley."

CHAPTER
Nine

KAT CONCENTRATED ON putting one foot in front of the other. Her mind still wasn't functioning very well. Considering how wrong she was every time she thought she knew what Moss was up to, she wasn't sure if that was a disadvantage or not. She wasn't even sure why she was following him up the steep wooden staircase, except that she trusted him. She wasn't at all sure she trusted herself.

For a moment there, she reflected, she'd even imagined he'd sounded pleased she was in the same profession he was. She wasn't just losing her mind; she'd obviously already lost it if she thought he might actually approve of her being a private investigator! It simply wasn't possible. Virtually without exception, men were threatened, wary, even downright belligerent when women sought untraditional— that is, masculine—roles. They were never, ever pleased. They certainly never approved.

Kat's eyes widened as she followed Moss up into the attic loft. "Oh!" Her high heels sinking into deliciously thick chocolate-brown carpet, she clasped her hands over her mouth. One entire side of the soaring cathedral ceiling had been replaced by panels of glass, the clerestory windows revealing a universe of velvet black night sky.

"It's beautiful," Kat breathed, staring up at the Big Dipper.

Moss came up behind her and rested his hands on her shoulders. "I thought you'd like it."

"Like it?" Kat protested, supremely aware of the warm fingers almost absently massaging the tense tendons at the base of her neck. "I love it! If it were mine, I wouldn't be able to resist sleeping up here every night. It'd be like literally sleeping under the stars."

"It is," Moss agreed, "and I do. Every night."

Stepping away, Kat turned slowly, her eyebrows arcing accusingly. "I thought you said your bedroom was downstairs."

White teeth flashed against Moss's deeply tanned face. "I lied. I was afraid you wouldn't come up if I told you the truth. How about some music?" As he talked he walked to the impressive bank of stereo equipment covering one wall.

Kat decided she was beginning to admire his incorrigibility much more than she should. Shaking her head at herself as much as at him, she watched him flip through a large array of albums and secretly found herself hoping he'd pick something bracing and wholly unromantic, like a Sousa march. Her fleeting wish died, and her confusion grew, when he placed a classical piece—Pachelbel's Canon in D—on the turntable. She'd thought she had Moss all figured out, was so sure she knew exactly what kind of man he was. But in truth, she realized, she didn't really know him at all.

"Nickel for your thoughts," he murmured, coming forward and handing her a bulbous brandy snifter filled with a respectable amount of the aromatic amber liquid.

Kat took a tentative sip of the potent liquor, savoring its warmth as it slid smoothly down her dry throat. "Whatever happened to a penny?"

"Inflation," said Moss gravely. He dropped down onto an enormous fur-covered beanbag chair and patted the spot beside him. "Come sit down."

Kat eyed the amorphous chair. "Are you going to behave yourself?"

Moss smiled serenely up at her. "Don't I always?"

"Ask a silly question . . ." Hesitating, Kat sat cautiously on the fur-covered chair. It moved almost sensuously as her weight settled into its softness, forming to the contours of her body like a warm cocoon.

Moss immediately shifted, and she involuntarily rolled up against him. "That's better." He smiled in satisfaction into her startled eyes. "Tell me, do you prefer to be called Kat?" He lifted his glass to his lips. "Or Katrina?"

Her thigh intimately pressed against his warmer, rock-hard one, Kat tore her eyes away from the lean brown fingers curled around his glass and tried to control her thundering pulse. Dear Lord, she thought in growing alarm, I really am head over heels in love with him! Either that, she concluded, or she was having heart trouble. No one had ever made her feel so ridiculously out of breath, so totally out of control. She wanted him, wanted him as she'd never wanted anyone in her life. But was that really love, she wondered, or just plain old-fashioned lust?

She was silent so long Moss asked wryly, "Don't tell me that's a secret, too?"

"No." Kat shook her head, trying to regain some of her usually reliable composure. "You're just the first man who ever asked. I think I'm in shock." Or in love. Which?

"Your ex called you Katrina tonight," he noted.

Kat looked down at her glass. "Derek always called me Katrina. He thought Kat sounded too unfeminine."

"Did he think being a private eye was unfeminine, too?"

"Of course." Kat looked up. "Don't you?"

Moss shrugged, swirling his glass. "I've never thought of professions as innately feminine or masculine."

"But you wouldn't go so far as to call me feminine, would you?" Kat challenged, unable to abandon the subject now that they were finally on it. "I mean, I'm hardly the soft, round, cuddly type who inspires a man to feel protective."

There was something going on behind those hot gray

eyes of his, but she was damned if she knew what.

"Searching for compliments, Kat?" He took a long sip of his brandy and watched her steadily over the rim of the glass.

"No," she said honestly, "just the truth." One way or the other, she had to know.

Moss's mouth curved with lazy sensuality. "You want the truth, Kat? All right, I'll give it to you." Kat felt his arm slide down around her shoulders. "The truth is that I don't find soft, round, cuddly women who need protecting particularly attractive. I like mine lean and healthy and fit and intelligent, capable of thinking on their feet." His arm tightened. "Satisfied?" he added, a trace of indulgent humor lacing his deep voice.

Actually, she wasn't. Convinced he was merely being tactful, not truthful, Kat pressed, "You don't think Derek's companion tonight was desirable?"

"She's pretty," Moss admitted readily, pulling Kat steadily closer, "but I doubt she's even half as interesting as you are." Moving carefully, almost as if she were a wild creature he was afraid of startling, he took the glass of brandy from Kat's unsteady fingers and set it, along with his, on a nearby end table.

"But my karate," she persisted as he turned back toward her. "Doesn't it bother you?" She refused to believe it didn't matter. It had been the kiss of death for Derek.

"Do I look bothered?"

No, Kat admitted to herself in confusion as she studied his tanned, angular face in the pale light. He looked more intrigued than disturbed by the evening's revelations. He certainly didn't look threatened. But was he really as calm and accepting as he seemed, or was he simply seeing what she so desperately wanted to see?

"But, Moss—" she began.

Before she could form her next question, his right hand had cupped her cheek, his thumb tracing her mouth, effectively sealing her lips.

"Are you always going to be this chatty when I try to make love to you?" he asked with mild interest.

Alarmed at the immediate response singing through her body at his touch, Kat strove for matching flippancy. "I don't know. Are you going to try to make love to me often?"

"Oh, yes," he promised with a seductive smile. "Very, very often. Starting now." As Kat gasped in surprise and pleasure, he rolled deftly on top of her, his considerable weight pinning her down into the forgiving softness of the beanbag chair.

The entire length of her body seemed to absorb and reflect the heat of his. Wildly aware of the very male hardness pressing against her pelvis, Kat instinctively shifted position and found herself in an even more compromising situation, with Moss's increasing state of arousal sending tremors of desire all the way down to her curled toes.

"Do that again," he urged, bracing himself on his elbows so that his smoldering gray eyes were barely an inch from her own.

Her ability to think sharply curtailed, Kat licked her dry lips and tried, unsuccessfully, to ignore her body's clamoring for even more intimacy with his.

"I feel it only fair to warn you," she said with a last-ditch effort at self-control, "that I'm not very good at this."

"I'll take my chances." Lifting the heavy silk fall of her hair, Moss nuzzled her throat, dropping hungry kisses down her exposed throat. "Mmm, you smell delicious." He raised his head and rubbed his nose sensuously against hers. "Good enough to eat. What are you wearing?"

"Cinnabar," Kat told him breathlessly, supremely aware of his mouth, so close to hers, the warmth of his breath fanning her face.

"*Sin* again." He sounded amused. "I can see I'm going to have to watch out for you. You're a very dangerous lady."

But not half as dangerous as he was, Kat reflected as the mouth hovering just above hers dropped down fractionally, still not quite touching hers but so close she could feel its scorching heat on hers.

"Moss." She automatically whispered, the threads of awareness binding them together almost suffocating in their intensity. "Moss, we shouldn't—"

"Probably not," he agreed, his voice as low as hers, so soft she could barely hear him, "but when the hell have either of us done what we should?"

Kat's hands tightened convulsively on his shoulders as he loosened the silky fabric of her tunic and nimbly unfastened the front clasp of her bra, pushing it gently aside. His fingers traced an invisible line across her bared collarbone into the cleft between her breasts.

"It's impossible to make love on a beanbag chair," she protested with another weak attempt at sanity.

"Challenging," Moss corrected, kissing the fragrant softness of her breasts and exploring the warm path of downy skin leading to her navel. "Not impossible."

"Ah." Kat seized almost desperately on the remark. "And what real man doesn't love a challenge, right?"

Moss stopped nuzzling her navel and lifted his gilded head. His steady gaze met hers, while Kat tried awkwardly to think of something to say. She'd been joking, chattering nervously because she was afraid to demonstrate to Moss just how inept at lovemaking she really was, but he seemed to take the unthinking comment seriously.

"That remark," he said quietly, "just slipped out tonight. I know it sounded patronizing, but it was either that or belt that smug ex-husband of yours, I'm afraid. I didn't think you'd want to be the object of a public brawl," he added, scanning her passion-flushed face.

"Oh, I don't know," Kat quipped, feeling her whole body quicken at the almost tangible touch of the visual caress. "I've never been brawled over. Sounds interesting."

At last he seemed to recognize the nervousness that compelled her to keep talking. He smiled with sudden knowledge. "You're not going to keep delaying the inevitable, are you?"

Feeling like a kitten who'd just tapped a much larger, infinitely more dangerous cat on the nose just a touch too sharply, Kat countered breathlessly, "What, precisely, is the inevitable?"

"If you don't already know," Moss mused, his eyes positively smoking with desire, "I guess it's high time I showed you."

His thumbs beneath her chin, he cupped her face in his large hands, gently forcing her trembling mouth up to meet his.

"Kat honey," he murmured against her tightly sealed lips, "unless you've got braces on, I want in there."

Kat instinctively opened her mouth in protest. "I told you I wasn't—" She remembered how sneaky he was, too late.

Submerged in a pool of silvery heat, Kat knew as soon as his mouth captured hers that making love with Moss was going to be different from anything she'd ever experienced. As his long, strong fingers brushed the delicate skin of her throat, she instinctively parted her lips in unconscious invitation. With a low groan, Moss slipped his tongue into the moist warmth of her mouth in a sensuous exploration that left Kat, this time, truly breathless.

Kat clutched his broad shoulders, holding him tight, drawing him closer and still closer until his hard thighs were pressed against the softness of hers. Her legs entangled with his longer ones, she reveled in the weight of his lean body as it rubbed enticingly, maddeningly over hers. Literally kissing her senseless, he lovingly stroked and caressed the fullness of her breasts, his mouth capturing then leaving hers, teasing her with tantalizing kisses in heretofore uncharted regions of her quivering body until the confining clothing separating her heated skin from his was as frustrating to her as it apparently was to him. Balked by the layers of silk, cotton, and wool between them, he swore softly.

"I think the problem here," he growled huskily against her throat, "is that we've both got far too many clothes on."

Feeling happy, desired, and incredibly sexy, Kat asked in a throaty whisper, "What do you suggest we do about it?"

His smile was deliciously evil. "I suggest we get naked."

In less than twenty seconds they were, as Moss's shirt

and slacks and Kat's silky tunic pajamas slid to the floor in a tumbled heap.

"Ah," Moss sighed in satisfaction as he pulled her down beneath him on the carpet. "That's much better." He kissed the satiny curve of her bare shoulder, playfully nibbling the sensitive skin with his teeth. "Mmm. You taste as good as you look."

He continued the exploration across her collarbone in a slow, erotic descent, teasing and tasting her inch by inch, lazily licking her down to her toes and back again, concentrating on the secret warmth between her legs until Kat, moaning in pleasure, half gasped, half pleaded, "Moss, please, you're driving me crazy!"

Prolonging the sweet torment, Moss switched his attention to the inside of her left thigh, tracing small, provocative patterns up her sensitized skin until Kat was certain she was going to explode from sheer ecstasy. Tremors rippled through her body.

"Moss? Moss!"

"Do you want me to stop?" he asked innocently without pausing in his explorations.

"What I want," said Kat fervently, lacing her fingers through his clean gold hair and urging him upward, "is for you to take me. Now. Please. Before I do something desperate."

"Well." At last Moss lifted his head, his eyes gleaming with desire and devilment. "Why didn't you say so?"

And as Kat let out a sigh of exasperation, he slid up her in one swift, powerful move, joining his body with hers, changing her sigh to one of pure pleasure as finally they were one.

Moving slowly at first, then more quickly, their bodies melded together in a wild, sweet dance of abandon. With Kat beneath Moss and then above him, they rolled across the thick carpet, laughing, loving, teasing with rapaciously thorough explorations of each other's bodies. Because of his greater weight and long reach, Moss had the unequivocal advantage. But Kat, her palms planted firmly against the muscle-hard wall of his tanned chest, repeatedly eluded his devouring mouth. Turning her head from side to side, she placed maddeningly short kisses on his seeking lips until, at last, in a frenzy of uncontrolled passion, he settled himself decisively on top, pinning her to the floor, capturing her mouth with his in a searing, penetrating kiss that had Kat clinging to him, whispering his name over and over again as they hurtled through the velvet blackness of space, crested the moon, rushed headlong past the stars. And then, with one last flare of explosive brightness, they slowly tumbled back to earth.

"Kat, my sweet Kat. You're so beautiful. So beautiful."

Utterly contented, Kat lay cradled in Moss's strong, warm arms, listening to his murmured words of loving praise and affection. Slowly, gently, his large hands traversed the length of her body to settle on the gentle flare of her hips, soothing her, reassuring her . . .

Finally, after a very long time, he leaned over and kissed her temple. "Happy?"

Turning her head, Kat smiled at him. "Oh, yes." Sighing, she stroked her hands lightly over his perspiration-dampened back, loving the feel of hard muscle and bone, the smooth texture of his skin.

"It was okay?" he teased.

"It was wonderful. No"—she smiled shyly into the curve of his shoulder—"it was better than wonderful. It was unbelievable. I never knew loving could be so much fun." Her head pillowed on his arm, Kat reached up and lovingly touched her palm to his cheek. "Oh, Moss. It's going to be so very, very nice being with you, loving with you, working together with you—"

Kat was vaguely aware that Moss's rough fingers, tracing a pattern over her hipbone, had suddenly stilled.

"Who," he said, very carefully, "said anything about working together?"

CHAPTER
Ten

KAT FELT AS if someone had dumped a bucket of cold water over her. She looked into Moss's face and found herself staring into gray eyes that seemed, for once, cool and not the least bit inviting.

"But this business at Mark's studio. I assumed . . . I thought . . . you . . . I . . . we . . ." Faltering under his total lack of encouragement, Kat forged on, "Aren't we going to pool our information? Work on it together?"

Moss shook his head slowly but emphatically. "No way. You're off the case, Kat. There's no need for both of us to be working on it."

"No need!" Pushing his hand off her hips, Kat sat up, pulling her discarded tunic top around her. "There's every need! I thought you understood." She stared at his impassive features, then continued, her words clipped and angry. "Have I been imagining things all night, or didn't you tell me earlier you knew how hard it was to get established in this business?" she demanded, knowing full well that wasn't the issue at all. The issue was whether or not he would accept her as an equal.

"You weren't imagining things." His voice was steady. "I just think you could find a better case to get established with."

"I don't want a better case!" Kat hissed. "I want this one. There's no reason we can't work on it together," she added.

"Yes, there is. I don't want to." Propped up on one elbow, Moss tried to draw her toward him, but Kat moved farther away.

"Don't you touch me, you . . . you traitor." She pulled the silky folds of her tunic tightly around her, irritated at herself as much as at him. Despite her anger, she was finding it almost impossible to control her physical reaction to him. Tearing her eyes away from the gloriously nude male body stretched out before her, she backed up another six inches for good measure.

Accepting her resistance, at least for the time being, Moss handed her the lacy briefs she'd surreptitiously been searching for and asked calmly, "Tell me why I'm a traitor."

Accepting the panties with as much dignity as she could muster, Kat snapped, "You know why. You let me believe you liked women who were independent, but the truth is you're as much a believer in the 'Me Tarzan, you Jane' approach to life as the next man. You like women to be independent only when it's convenient. Which, by your standards, isn't very often."

"I see. You're assuming I want you off the case because you're a woman," said Moss, looking thoughtful.

"I'm not *assuming* anything," Kat retorted loftily. "I'm going by experience."

"*Past* experience," Moss pointed out, "which means you're confusing me with your ex-husband again, when in fact he and I are nothing alike."

Kat gave him a look of patent disbelief. "Really."

Looking exasperated, Moss pinched the bridge of his nose. "I wish to hell you'd never met him."

Kat smiled grimly. "That makes two of us."

"At last." Moss's own smile was bleakly amused. "We agree on something." When Kat refused to respond, he let out a heavy sigh. "Look, Kat, believe me when I say my decision has nothing whatsoever to do with your sex. I always work alone. I've never had a partner."

"So change!"

"I don't want to change," he said flatly. "I work best alone. Always have. Try being a little more reasonable, will you?"

More reasonable? He meant more submissive, and they both knew it!

Self-disgust welled up inside Kat. How could she possibly have been so stupid? Whatever had made her think Moss was any different from any other man? That he was any different from Derek? And why should it matter so damned much that he wasn't?

Because she felt betrayed. She'd made love with Moss not just because she was attracted to him, not just because she was in love with him, but because she'd been so sure he not only desired and wanted her but accepted her for what she was. She'd been searching for a man like that all her life.

Tonight, feeling confident she'd found him at last, she'd discarded her fears and reservations and bared herself, body and soul. She'd seen their lovemaking as a commitment, as the sealing of a bond, as the beginning of a partnership both personal and professional. But it had all, apparently, been an illusion on her part.

And now? Now she was hurt and angry and didn't give two hoots and a holler whether she was being reasonable or not. Moss was really no different from Derek, she decided. He was threatened by her, all right. He just hid it better.

She eyed Moss's prone form with a mixture of murder and mayhem. "I suppose *you* think it's reasonable to refuse to work with me just because my name is Kat and not Carl?"

"I've already told you it's not because you're a woman—" Moss began mildly.

"I know what you told me," Kat cut him off. "I don't believe you."

Moss opened his mouth, changed his mind, and shut it again. Assessing her grim expression for a moment, he rose lithely and began to search out his clothes. Stubbornly refusing to let herself be unnerved by the sheer beauty of his nude, muscular body, Kat silently handed him his dark blue briefs and ignored the seductive gleam in his eyes as he reached down and helped her up.

It was quite impossible to ignore the waves of hot silver rushing through her constricted veins as he bent over and pulled the briefs up his long, tanned legs. Abruptly turning her back to him, Kat jerked on her panties, resolutely telling herself that once they were both safely dressed again her heart would stop its ridiculous thundering.

"Don't you think you're overreacting just a little?" Moss asked, sounding infuriatingly reasonable when he was being anything but.

"I don't think it's possible to overreact in this situation." Tugging her braided belt around her waist, Kat took a deep, bolstering breath and started to turn around again, only to find that Moss had moved even closer to her in the interim. Her nose was practically touching his bare chest. She felt her heart slam up and down and then finally lodge in her throat. Panicked, she started to take a step backward. With infinite calm, Moss halted her progress. Placing her hands firmly on her shoulders, he pulled her against him, capturing her within the circle of his arms.

Kat resisted a moment longer, then with a groan of surrender, slid her arms around his narrow waist. Inhaling his erotically earthy scent, she buried her face against his chest and felt the warmth of his bare skin enfold her.

"Damn you," she said, and she heard Moss's soft laugh of understanding.

"That's honest, at least." He held her tightly, as if trying to banish the rift between them. For a long time neither of them moved or spoke, clinging together as if threatened by an outside force. Finally he rubbed his chin slowly across the top of Kat's bent head. "Tell me exactly what it is you want from this relationship of ours so we can get this problem cleared up once and for all."

"What problem?" Kat countered with distinct reluctance, willing to let sleeping dogs lie. At least for the moment.

"Kat..."

At Moss's growled warning, Kat lifted her tousled head, met his eyes, and answered carefully, "What I want is for you to accept me as a woman but not a helpless one. I want you to accept that I'm capable of defending myself if necessary. And I want you to accept that I'm a competent investigator."

"I do accept all those things."

"Then let me work on this case with you!" Kat tried gamely to smile but failed in the attempt when, for the second time that evening, Moss shook his head.

"Forget it, Kat. You're off the case."

"Wait a minute. You can't mean...you're not saying I'm off the case completely, just that I can't work with you. Right?" Kat's widened eyes begged him to agree. He didn't.

"Why?" she demanded. "Because you're afraid I'll solve this case before you do?" She extricated herself from his embrace.

"If you want to think that," said Moss, looking unperturbed, "go ahead. Just stay off the case."

The trouble was, she *didn't* want to think that. She wanted to believe he had some ulterior motive. But what? If he believed she was as competent as he professed, then that, she decided, should be that. "I have just as much right to work this case as you do," she insisted, her natural stubbornness coming into full play when faced with his continued intransigence.

"No, you don't. I was working on it a full week before you stepped into the picture. Haven't you ever heard of ethics?"

"Don't you talk to me about ethics!" Kat railed at him. "We're talking about survival here!"

"I couldn't agree more," muttered Moss, but Kat had already turned away, engaged in a brisk search for the remainder of her outfit.

She blinked rapidly, fighting the tears that threatened to spill down her cheeks. "Have you seen my—Ah, there they are." She extracted her trousers from beneath the beanbag chair and swiftly pulled them on. She was not going to cry, she was not . . .

"What are you doing?"

"Leaving." Futilely, Kat searched for her shoes. "I'm not staying where I'm not wanted." A faint snuffle marred the calm effect she was trying to project.

Moss reached out and snagged her wrist, dragging her toward him. "You're wanted. Oh, lady, how you're wanted." Crushing her to him to prevent her escape, he nibbled on her earlobe while his hands went on an exploration of their own.

"Moss!" Kat gasped, sucking in her breath as his questing fingers slid inside the elastic waistband of her loosely fitting pajama trousers. "Stop that! This isn't going to solve . . . I'm not going to . . . No! I just put those on . . . you can't . . ."

Silk whispered to the floor, and Kat moaned, her protests fading, then disappearing altogether as Moss's hands divested her of her lacy black panties. His long fingers cupped her bottom, lifting her upward until her slender legs wound around his waist, locking them together.

"You're terrible," she groaned into the curve of his neck. "We ought to be talking, not making love."

"Sometimes," Moss growled, "I think we talk too damned much."

His hands swiftly went to work to undo her tunic. Kat clung to him, lowering each arm obediently as he removed the offending garment and dropped it onto the floor.

Moving his hips seductively beneath her, his hands closed over her bared breasts, his thumbs gently rubbing their pink tips.

"Oh, Lord," Kat moaned, planting kisses across his broad shoulders and down the hollow of his collarbone. "How am I supposed to have any self-control, let alone any self-righteous anger, when you do that?"

"You mean this?" Laughing softly, Moss shifted his narrow hips once more, settling her more firmly on top of him. "Or this?" His large hands tightened possessively on her breasts.

With a quick intake of breath, Kat arched against him, her body seeking fullfillment. Her hands dropped to the cotton briefs still separating them, but Moss held her back.

Reaching up, he wiped the remaining dampness from her cheeks. "I love you, sweetheart." His deep voice was husky with emotion.

"I love you, too," Kat admitted, her voice equally husky.

"Then don't worry. We can work this thing out."

Kat moved, uncertain how to voice her misgivings. But her shift in position heightened Moss's smoldering passion to the searing point before she could speak. He lowered her quickly to the floor, her legs still binding them together as he lay on top of her.

"Dear God, I want you," he groaned against her bare skin. "Do you want me?" His hands moved over her hips.

"Yes," Kat breathed. "Oh, yes."

"Then show me."

But even as she did, Kat knew their problems weren't about to end at all. They were, she was certain, just beginning.

Kat spent most of Monday morning cleaning out her desk and 1) trying to explain to Mark why she'd lied about her qualifications in the first place—after promising Moss she would—and 2) attempting to explain why she couldn't stay now that the truth was out.

As mornings went, she decided, it was the absolute pits.

First she'd stumbled through her confession like an idiot. And then, as she'd suspected he might, Mark, in a lamentable effort at gallantry, offered to keep her on as his secretary after agreeing with Moss—probably for the first time in his life—that she couldn't ethically continue to work on the case he'd asked Moss to solve.

For one brief, crazy moment Kat had been tempted to take him up on his offer. But knowing Moss would guess, correctly, that she wouldn't be able to keep her fingers out of the pie as long as she was within reaching distance, she'd finally decided against it. Moss was just ruthless enough to throw her out, quite literally, on her derrière.

And so she was now at home, off the case both officially and unofficially. And she was feeling lost, depressed, and decidedly disgusted with herself.

With perfectly awful timing, Ken had left the day before for a twice-yearly trek to Los Angeles to visit an old college friend. Alone, and for once lonely, Kat settled herself on her living-room couch and picked up a book she'd been dying to read. Four minutes later she put it down unread.

It wasn't her unemployment that was getting her down, she concluded; it was the way Moss had gotten her to agree to lay off the case. So what if he'd professed his love at precisely the moment she was most vulnerable? So what if she'd agreed during the heat of passion to no longer thwart him by working on the case in secret? That didn't necessarily mean he'd purposefully squashed her resistance with love-making, didn't mean he'd used her obvious attraction to him to get his way.

Or did it?

Kat picked up her cup of coffee—her sixth so far that day—and studied its murky depths. Moss had said he loved her, had said he wanted her. Why was she having so much trouble believing the former but not the latter? Because she was an insecure idiot, that's why. She was out of work and out of sorts and definitely wallowing in self-pity. It was obviously going to be a very long day.

The only thing that livened it up, loosely speaking, was her running battle with her new next-door neighbor. Mr. Barker, a cranky old man who was obviously not aging gracefully, preferred—no, demanded—funereal silence. If Kat forgot and slammed a door, he pounded on the wall. If she let her teakettle whistle for more than three seconds straight, he rapped on the wall. Of course, playing her stereo was out of the question.

Kat tried hard to be patient. She closed cupboards carefully, refrained from wearing her favorite clogs, played her bedside radio on the lowest volume.

Mr. Barker thumped on the wall.

Kat supposed at any other time it might seem funny, but today she wasn't laughing at much of anything. Something was going to have to give. In a moment of pure inspiration, she decided to have a heart-to-heart talk with him. He refused to answer his door. And someone with his delicate hearing didn't have a telephone. Naturally.

The time for action, she concluded, had come. Unfortunately, she didn't know what kind of action to take. Calling the police seemed like such a petty thing to do. Complaining to the landlord likewise. After all, the man was in his eighties. For all she knew, driving her crazy was his sole source of entertainment.

She was probably overreacting, she decided. Maybe when her sense of humor returned . . . ? On that optimistic thought, Kat grabbed her purse and jacket and headed out the door, closing it softly behind her. Whistling under her breath, feeling in control of her life again, she was halfway to her beloved old Toyota when she stopped in mid-stride.

All four tires had been slashed.

Stunned, Kat scanned the street and saw that nobody else's tires were damaged. Evidently she had been the target of somebody's ill temper, and it didn't take any crystal ballgazing to guess who the culprit was.

Balefully eyeing her neighbor's shaded windows, Kat let herself back into her apartment and stomped to the kitchen to make herself her seventh cup of coffee for the day. Her mind was forming sinister thoughts about unsocial neighbors when Mark chose that moment to call.

"Hi, Katrina. How are things going?"

Ordinarily, Kat would have said things were fine whether they were or not, but she was so irritated about her car that she ended up mentioning the slashed tires. Before she could explain about her less-than-friendly neighbor, Mark jumped to the obvious, if erroneous, conclusion that it was connected with the incidents at his studio.

"Maybe you ought to call Moss," he said, sounding more concerned than she'd ever heard him. "Better to be safe than sorry."

Why he thought she'd be safe with Moss around, Kat had no idea. Moss's presence would simply change the source of danger. If, in fact, she was presently in danger, which she sincerely doubted.

"Mark," she said patiently, "Moss is *your* big brother, not mine. I'd feel silly calling him. What am I supposed to say, that I'm afraid of being alone in the dark?"

She heard him sigh. "I suppose you're right. But I'd feel a lot better if I hadn't insisted on hiring you. If anything happens, I'm going to feel responsible. Do take care, Katrina, won't you?"

Kat assured him she would. Unfortunately, Ken wasn't so easily dispensed with. Needing someone sane to talk to, she'd called to tell him he'd received a package in the mail and she'd picked it up for him. He'd recognized the tension in her voice and soon had the whole story wangled out of her.

"I don't suppose you've called Moss Adams and told him any of this," her brother said as Kat rubbed her forehead in irritation.

"I don't need—"

"Never mind," Ken cut her off. "I'll call him myself. You wouldn't be in danger if I hadn't opened my big mouth—"

"Oh, for goodness sake! Ken—"

"You sit tight and keep the door locked until Moss gets in touch with you," he commanded, sounding uncharacteristically firm. He refused to hang up until she'd promised.

Exactly three minutes and thirty-three seconds after she'd replaced the receiver, the telephone rang. Distinctly reluctant to answer it, Kat listened to it shrill. Two rings. Three rings. When she finally picked it up she knew exactly whose voice she was going to hear on the other end.

"I've just finished talking to both our brothers," Moss said, sounding as calm as Mark and Ken had sounded anxious. "How about telling me exactly what happened?"

Letting out a moan of exasperation, Kat repeated what she'd told their respective siblings, this time explaining about her neighbor Mr. Barker. Kat was certain Moss would agree with her that it was all much ado about nothing.

He didn't. He was silent for so long, Kat thought they'd been disconnected. "I don't like the sound of that," he said at last.

It was, Kat knew by now, a gross understatement. She'd never met anyone who could put so much meaning into so few words.

In a way she was glad she hadn't told him about the dead mouse she'd discovered on the front seat of her car two days ago. Then she'd thought it had merely been left by a mischievous cat. Now she wasn't so sure. In any case, she knew exactly how Moss would view the incident.

"I really don't think there's anything to worry about," she said firmly. Mr. Barker was certainly an unpleasant fellow, but she doubted he went in for physical attacks. He was, after all, eighty years old. Besides, she was bigger than he was.

"You don't know that. The guy is obviously unbalanced. He could be dangerous." There was a brief pause. Kat heard Moss light a cigarette and exhale, puzzled because she would've sworn he didn't smoke. "I think I'd better come over tonight," he said after a moment. "I'll check this Mr. Barker out in the morning."

Her nerves tingling wildly at the thought of Moss spending the night, Kat said with attempted humor, "Are you coming over to protect my body or preside over it?"

She could almost hear the ill-advised joke land with a thud.

"If you're worried about my intentions," said Moss, steel encasing every syllable, "I'll check you into a hotel. Alone."

So much for the light approach, Kat decided with a wince. "I'm not going anywhere," she asserted. Still smarting from the small verbal slap he'd just delivered, she added just a touch spitefully, "Don't you think you're overreacting just a little?"

Silence. A full ten seconds of it. "No," he said, "I don't."

Kat took a deep breath and tried cajoling him instead. "Moss, this is ridiculous. I told you before, I don't need babysitting. I'm sorry I even mentioned the tires to Mark. And Ken has always been overprotective. Why don't we just forget the whole thing? I'll be fine. Really. Believe me, I can take care of myself."

On the whole, Kat decided later, it was probably one of the stupidest statements she'd ever made.

She'd already turned on the shower and had one foot in when she remembered that she'd forgotten to lock the front door after promising both Ken and Moss she would. Leaving the water on and closing the bathroom door behind her to keep the steam in, Kat belted the yellow terry-cloth robe around her waist and walked back toward the living room. Standing in the doorway, she surveyed the darkened room before her in puzzlement. She distinctly remembered leaving the lights on. Cautiously feeling her way to the table lamp nearest her, she flicked it on. Nothing happened. Odd, she thought. She'd just replaced that particular bulb only last week.

Feeling vaguely like the intrepid heroine in an improbable horror flick, Kat felt her way toward the unlocked front door, deciding she'd change the light bulb later. She was a third of the way across the blackened room when the floor creaked.

Kat had lived in the apartment long enough to know every squeaky board by heart. And she wasn't standing on one of them.

Her heart increased its tempo. You're being silly and paranoid, she told herself firmly. But she stood very still, listening, all the same.

At the second creak, Kat knew she wasn't alone. Someone was moving around in the kitchen. Stealthily.

Muscles tensed, she listened to the floor squeak a third time. By now she was barely breathing. She really ought to be doing *something*, she concluded. But what? The phone wasn't in the kitchen, so calling Moss or the police was a possibility. Of course, she could always confront the burglar . . . No, that was ridiculous. What on earth would a burglar be looking for in the kitchen? So, if not a burglar, who? Mr. Barker? Surely that cranky old man knew that slashing tires was one thing, but breaking and entering . . .

A drawer in the kitchen opened, and on the other side
of their thin, shared wall Kat heard Mr. Barker flushing his
toilet. It struck her with the force of an sledgehammer. If
Mr. Barker was in his apartment, who was in her kitchen?

Kat had been annoyed as long as she thought it was the
old man setting out to play some sort of prank—rubber
snakes in the cupboards or something equally harmless—
but not frightened.

She was frightened now.

Memories of another time, not quite two years ago, when
she'd come upon another midnight intruder, flooded through
her mind. And suddenly she was shaking all over. Long-
healed scars reopened, and she was reliving the nightmare,
re-experiencing the savage beating, feeling every blow . . .

She had to get out. But how? The only door to the
apartment was closer to the kitchen than to where she was
standing. And it would do no good to go in the other direction. The lock on the bathroom door was broken.

Kat backed up, feeling cornered, feeling the panic surging up inside her like some terrible volcanic force. As she
moved, the boards beneath her bare feet creaked, sounding
like a gunshot in the stillness.

Kat stopped breathing. She could almost hear the intruder
pausing, listening. The only sound filling the silence was
the faint rush of water running in the shower. Then she
heard it. Footsteps. Quiet, stealthy ones, moving slowly,
purposefully toward the kitchen door from the other side.

Kat bit her lower lip until she could taste blood. What
in heaven's name was she going to do? No track star, she
doubted she could make it to the front door without being
cut off before she reached it. She wasn't even sure her shaky
legs would carry her that far.

The slow, steady creak of the kitchen door opening sent
fear rising in Kat's throat like mercury in a thermometer on
a hot day. Without making the conscious decision to flee,
she stumbled in the direction of the entry door, seeking
escape.

Panicked and disoriented in the dark, she moved too far
to the left. Her foot snagged the edge of the carpet, tripping

her. She fell heavily to her knees.

With a whimper of rising hysteria, Kat clawed her way back to her feet. Bumping into something sharply, she was conscious of a table not being where she thought it ought to be a split second before the rush of cool air licked over her skin like a thousand fluttering bats.

And then she felt the crushing impact of something hard and solid and deadly slamming against her chest. And she fell, unconscious, to the floor.

CHAPTER

Eleven

LEAD WEIGHED DOWN her eyelids. Something cool and hard pressed against her back. Deep in the recesses of Kat's mind it registered that she could feel her fingers and toes, even if she couldn't seem to move them.

At least, she decided, that meant she wasn't dead. She hoped.

She forced her eyelids open. They fluttered against the bright glare of an overhead light, then dropped to slits. She saw Moss's blurred form kneeling over her, heard the slow, even sound of his breathing. The sound of her own breathing was decidedly lacking.

She was just beginning to wonder why, when Moss slipped his strong hands under her waist and lifted her upward, forcing her back to arch slightly. Kat gasped for air.

"Take it easy. Try to breathe slow and deep."

Kat would have been happy to breathe at all. The pain below her rib cage was all-consuming. She felt as if she'd run into a moving train . . . and the train had won.

Moss lifted her body again, forcing her lungs to expand.

"That hurts," Kat protested futilely.

"It ought to. You'll have bruised ribs for a while, but nothing appears to be broken. Lie still." Moss pushed her back down as she struggled to sit up. "You're not going anywhere, yet."

That much, at least, was true. Kat lay back and closed her eyes, waiting for the throbbing pain in her head to subside. Lord, she felt as if someone had whapped her over the head with a two-by-four. She reached up tentatively to find out why and discovered a hard knot the size of a small plum on the back of her head.

"You hit the floor when you went down," Moss said, lighting a cigarette. He sat down next to her, watching her dispassionately as she struggled to breathe normally. "Next time, try turning on the lights."

Kat stared at the ceiling. Was he angry with her for some reason? She hadn't exactly expected him to cover her with comforting kisses; he wasn't the type. But she hadn't expected him to be totally unsympathetic, either.

She licked her lips. They felt dry and cracked. "I didn't fall down. Someone was here. They . . . they knocked me down."

She saw the flicker in Moss's gray eyes as he brought the cigarette to his lips a second time. "Who was it?"

Kat paused, her mind refusing to function clearly. "I don't know," she said at last. "It was dark. I couldn't see him."

"You said *him*. Was it a man?"

So she had. Kat shivered, suddenly cold. Her mind felt wrapped in filmy gauze.

"Why did you think it was a man?" Moss persisted.

Really, you'd think he wasn't interested in her welfare at all, Kat thought with a flash of annoyance. He sounded more interested in the intruder!

She struggled to a sitting position and leaned back against the wall. "I don't know. I just assumed it was a man." She started to tuck her robe around her legs and stared at her right hand. One knuckle was skinned and bleeding.

Moss handed her a folded white handkerchief. "You didn't see his face?"

Kat took the cloth and pressed it against the wound. "No. But whoever it was, it wasn't a burglar."

"Are you sure?"

Kat bit her lower lip, which had unexpectedly started to tremble. "It wasn't a burglar," she repeated. Whoever it was had been trying to scare her . . . and had succeeded.

"It was probably just someone after your microwave."

"I don't have a microwave." Kat suppressed a shiver.

"An antique, then."

"I don't have any antiques." Kat's voice had risen. "And you can stop looking at me like I've gotten paranoid. I ought to know whether I was the target or not. You weren't here. It wasn't *you* who had the door slammed in your face!"

She blinked back tears. Why on earth didn't he hold her, comfort her, instead of simply looking at her with those ash-gray eyes as if he didn't believe a word she was saying? She knew exactly what had happened now. It was all coming back with a rush, and she was angry. Angry at having been frightened out of her wits. And angry at Moss for not seeming to care that she'd nearly gotten badly hurt—possibly killed—by her own sheer stupidity.

She jumped as Moss unfolded his great length and rose slowly to his feet. He threw his cigarette into the sink. "Got any booze?"

Kat kept a bottle of brandy above the fridge for when Ken came over. Moss reached up without stretching and brought it down. He put a pot of water on the stove and within minutes had her sitting down at the kitchen table with a steaming cup of black coffee in her hands. He laced it heavily with the brandy.

"Is this how you handle hysterical women?" Kat asked bitterly, wiping away her tears with the back of her hand. He was looking at her for further signs of an impending breakdown, and she knew it.

"All the time." Unperturbed, he sat down across from her and cradled his own mug in his large hands. Dressed in a black turtleneck sweater and black corduroy jeans, he looked tough and dangerous, almost broodingly handsome, and in complete control of his emotions. Kat wished she could say the same thing for herself. She felt—and probably looked—disheveled, disoriented, and not in control of anything, least of all her emotions.

Moss slipped a pack of cigarettes from his hip pocket. "How did this intruder of yours get in?" His eyes locked with hers over the flame of his lighter.

Wondering when on earth he'd started smoking, Kat swallowed two more sips of coffee before answering. "The front door. I hadn't remembered to lock it. That's where I was headed when he . . . when I . . ."

"And you didn't see what he looked like?"

Another surge of remembered fear shuddered through Kat. "No. I've already told you it was dark. Look"—she smiled tightly—"would you mind if we dropped the subject? I really don't want—"

"Was he big? Small? Come on, girl, you must have noticed at least that much." Moss drank from his mug, but his eyes were on her.

Anger, resentment, and fear all mingled together as Kat tried to control her strong desire to dissolve into a ranting, raving, hysterical mess of tears. "Didn't you hear me? I don't want to discuss it anymore!"

"It's not going to be any easier tomorrow," said Moss.

How the hell would he know? Kat leaned back in her chair, holding the coffee mug against her, letting the warmth of it seep through her thin bathrobe. She stared into the black brew and finally said, "I don't know what he looked like because I panicked. Happy now? It could have been a gorilla or one of the seven dwarfs for all I know. I was too busy trying to run for my life to notice. There, that ought to satisfy your curiosity. Now if you don't mind—"

She started to push away from the table. Moss hooked his foot under the seat of her chair, preventing her flight. "Are you mad at me or at yourself because you didn't act the way you think you should have?"

"I'm mad," Kat blazed, slamming her cup on the table, "because I behaved like an idiot! I totally panicked and forgot everything I ever learned about self-defense in my hurry to get away." Bitter disappointment lay on her tongue like ashes. It had been no better than that first time . . . No, this time had been worse, because *this* time she should've known what to do. And hadn't done it.

Moss lifted his shoulders. "So you ran. So you're not as brave as you thought you were. Most males find that out about themselves before they hit puberty."

Kat's teeth snapped together at the callous reply. "Don't you have even one sympathetic bone in your body?" she demanded. "I thought I was going to be killed! It's probably sheer luck I wasn't."

"But you weren't," he said with unanswerable logic, "were you?"

"No!" Kat winced as she spoke.

"Head hurt?"

"Yes!" she snapped and winced again.

"Got any aspirin?"

I don't want any aspirin, Kat wanted to shout at him. I want you to show me you understand, that you care.

"In the bathroom," she muttered.

Moss disappeared down the hall and returned with the bottle in his hand. He offered it to her with a glass of water. Kat shook out two tablets and swallowed them. She was setting down the glass when she looked up suddenly. And then she saw. Saw the look of concern in the smoky gray eyes and knew that he *did* understand and was treating her the way he'd expect to be treated after a similar experience. Would Moss have dissolved into tears because of a temporary lapse of judgment? No, he would not. He'd pick himself up, dust himself off. He wouldn't get mad; he'd get even. He certainly wouldn't quit.

Kat ran her forefinger around the rim of her cup. "When did you start smoking?" she asked, feeling a trickle of warmth slide through her veins at last. Was that a glimmer of self-mockery in his eyes? Yes, she was sure it was.

"The first time?" His mouth twisted. "When I was six-teen. I quit about four years ago. And started again," he admitted, she could have sworn reluctantly, "yesterday."

"Because you were worried about me," said Kat, certain she was right.

Moss snuffed out the half-smoked cigarette. "Going to take the blame for that, too?" His sudden, wry smile caught her off guard, and all at once she felt a kind of kinship with him that had nothing to do with her physical attraction to him.

He understood. He knew how it felt to let yourself down. He knew exactly how she felt, how stupid, how inadequate. And he was telling her, in his own way, that it would pass. That soon she would feel whole again. That the shattered illusions would mend—not without cracks perhaps—slowly and surely into something stronger, something more resilient.

Self-confidence, she decided, was a strange and wonderful thing. It could make you or break you. Hers had definitely taken a beating, maybe not quite so literally as it had in the past, but it had been in serious jeopardy of being destroyed. Moss, being the kind of man he was, had no qualms at all about helping her rebuild it.

"You never really thought it was a burgler at all, did you?" she asked, filled with a sense of wonder.

"No."

He'd simply been trying to get her back on her feet, and if that meant turning her fear into anger—even if it would be directed at him—he'd been willing to do it. Why? Because he loved her. Because her hurt was his hurt.

Love for him welled up inside Kat until she thought she would burst. She swallowed more of the coffee, her veins running with molten silver now.

"You believe this business tonight is connected with what's been going on at Mark's studio, don't you."

"I think it's a strong possibility."

Kat took a deep breath. "And you knew that something like this would happen eventually if I took the job as Mark's secretary," she reflected aloud, knowing now without a doubt that it had never been her competence or her femininity that had been in question. It had been her safety.

"I thought it might."

"And *that's* why you wanted me to work somewhere else. Why you wanted me off the case." Even with her muddled mind, she knew she was right. All the time she'd thought Moss had been patronizing her, what he'd been doing was worrying. About her.

"Yes."

"But why now? I quit working for Mark. And I certainly haven't been involved with him."

"You didn't have to be. All you had to do was be too inquisitive, too intelligent, and very, very observant."

"Not so observant." Kat eyed the kitchen door. But maybe too inquisitive, considering the number of people she'd talked with about Mark's problems at the studio. Too many to pinpoint any one person as a suspect. She looked at Moss. "Do you have any idea who the culprit is?"

"Not yet."

But he would. Somehow Kat didn't doubt that. Moss would be relentless, keeping at it until he found the source of the problems. Kat shuddered involuntarily. She wouldn't want to be that person when he found him.

Moss rose suddenly. He took both mugs to the sink, washed them, and set them on the drainboard. "I think it's time you hit the sack."

"I'm not sleepy," Kat protested.

"Do you want me to carry you into the bedroom," he asked calmly, "or would you prefer to walk?"

Handed that choice, Kat slowly got up from the table and, with Moss two steps behind her, walked to her bedroom. "Are you planning on tucking me in, too?" she asked seductively.

Moss was at the window, checking to see that it was locked. When he turned and looked at her, Kat's throat tightened.

"Behave yourself," he scolded. "You've had quite a shock tonight. Not to mention a nasty bump on the head. What you need is rest."

No, Kat corrected mentally, what she needed was him.

Slipping off her robe, she turned back the cool, flowered sheets and wondered what it would be like to be married to Moss, to live with him day after day. Beneath that cool facade lay a lot of smoldering emotions . . .

Feeling the hotness of his gaze on her, Kat turned around and realized for the first time that, except for her smile, she had nothing on.

"You've got exactly three seconds to climb into that bed," said Moss, "and cover yourself up. One, two . . ."

Making a small moue, Kat hopped into the bed and arranged the sheets so that she was covered all the way up to her flushed cheeks. "Thank you for turning off the shower," she said meekly.

"You're welcome."

With a last, long look at her, he headed for the door. Thinking he was leaving the apartment, Kat went into a new panic. "Moss, don't go!" She didn't want to be alone.

Moss stopped and turned around. "I wasn't leaving," he assured her quietly. "I was going to check the other windows. I'll sleep on the couch tonight."

Kat's relief was almost as strong as her disappointment. A week ago the thought of Moss sleeping in the next room would have given her a whopping case of insomnia. Tonight, his doing the very same thing would wreak the same kind of havoc on her sleeping habits, but for very different reasons.

His hand touched the doorknob.

"Moss?"

Once again he turned. Kat looked down, her fingers creasing the flowered sheet. "Would it help if I acted as . . . bait?"

For a moment she thought he wasn't going to answer. His hand remained on the doorknob. "You mean try to set a trap?"

Kat couldn't tell from his lack of inflection if he thought the idea was terrific or ridiculous. She nodded. "Yes."

Leaving the door, Moss walked over to the bed and sat down, his lean hip warm against her thigh. "Would you do that?"

Did he doubt she had the courage after tonight? Kat wondered. She could hardly blame him after the way she acted.

"I want to help," she said firmly, ignoring the small flutter of fear deep in her stomach. She needed to prove to herself, as much as to him, that she could do it. It was sort of like getting on a horse again once you'd fallen off, she reflected. It was now or never.

Moss let out a low sigh. "I don't know, Kat..."

The sudden appearance of tears sliding down her cheeks was as much a surprise to her as it apparently was to him. Kat tried to hold them back, to no avail. "I'm sorry." She attempted vainly to smile. "What were you going to say?"

Moss muttered something under his breath. With gentle fingers, he wiped the dampness from her cheeks. "Somehow tears are the last thing I expected from you."

"I'm not crying." Kat sniffed. "I've just got something in my eye."

"Hell." Moss gathered her into his arms, crushing her yielding body to his. "What am I going to do with you?"

"Make love to me," Kat suggested on a faint snuffle, her voice small and muffled against his shoulder. "I'll never get to sleep if you don't."

"I'll hold you," Moss growled, giving in, "until you go to sleep. And that's all, you shameless woman."

But, of course, that wasn't all. Only this time, Moss's lovemaking was slow and sweet and gentle and infinitely tender. And Kat fell asleep in his arms, safe and contented, reassured that somehow, some way, everything would be all right.

CHAPTER
Twelve

"WAKE UP, LAZYBONES. Another day has dawned."

Her face half-buried in her pillow, Kat opened one eyelid just enough to see Moss slip a covered tray onto the nightstand. "'S still night," she mumbled sleepily, vaguely aware that the room wasn't light yet.

"No, it's not." Moss sat on the edge of the bed and deftly rolled Kat onto her back, kissing the bare curve of her neck until she gave a low purr of pleasure. "Time to get up." He gave her a gentle shake when her eyes remained steadfastly shut.

"Come back to bed," she urged.

"If I come back to bed,"—Moss tweaked her ear—"neither of us will *ever* get up."

True. Stretching, Kat stifled a yawn. "What time is it?" she murmured drowsily, deliciously relaxed and perfectly content to stay precisely where she was.

"Five."

Kat's eyes flew open. Five? As in A.M.? She peered blearily at the bedside clock and fell back with a loud groan. Lord, no one but birds got up at such an hour! Muttering something unintelligible but nonetheless disparaging about morning people, Kat nestled deeper under the warm blankets, ignoring Moss's exaggerated sigh.

"I've reconsidered your offer of help," he told her, "and I've decided to accept."

That woke her up. "You have?"

"I have indeed. Coffee?"

"Please." Not quite sure how to take his calm expression, Kat started to sit up, then stopped. "Aaah." Every muscle in her body had awakened to protest the movement, reminding her of last night's close encounter with the door. Kat took a deep breath until the pain subsided, then tried again, moving more slowly this time. Feeling as if she were made of glass and was in danger of breaking, she leaned back against the pillow Moss had plumped for her.

"The day after is always the worst," he said, handing her a glass of orange juice and two aspirins. Downing the tablets, Kat handed back the empty glass and watched as Moss poured two cups of coffee. From the dampness of his dark gold hair, he'd obviously just come from the shower, and he was looking disgustingly chipper, she decided, considering when they'd both finally gotten to sleep the night before.

Taking the cup of coffee with a shy smile of thanks, Kat let the steam caress her flushed face for a moment as memories of Moss's lovemaking slid warmly through her mind. She'd been made love to before, but it had never, ever, been like that.

Hot waves of desire flickered through her as she relived every gentle stroke of Moss's hands, every lingering kiss, every murmured endearment. Moss had sensed her insecurity, her need to be reassured. He'd known exactly how frightened she'd been, how bruised she was in both body and soul . . . and had shown her in every way he could how much he loved her.

How she ever could have thought him ruthless, Kat didn't know.

She looked at him a moment and knew she was in love.

"Are you saying," she asked carefully, "you want me to act as bait?"

There was no doubt about it, she was thoroughly pleased and ridiculously flattered he wanted her to work with him. But at the same time, she was distinctly nervous at the prospect. What if she panicked again? She couldn't let Moss down!

Moss handed her a piece of buttered toast. "We can discuss details later. Are you still interested in helping?"

Kat bit into the toast, forcing herself to remain calm. She could do it, she knew she could, once she got over this awful, fluttery feeling of impending disaster. She smiled brightly. "Do chickens lay eggs?"

Moss ran a hand over his drying hair, looking unsurprised by her supposed readiness to jump into the fray. "That's what I figured. Would it do any good at all to suggest you be very careful?"

"I'm always careful!" Kat protested.

"That," said Moss, "was what I was afraid you'd say. You don't carry a gun by any chance?"

Kat smiled broadly at the too-casual-to-really-be-casual question. "Not me," she told him cheerfully. "The things scare me half to death. I'm a firm believer in hand-to-hand combat."

"That's what I thought."

Kat couldn't tell whether he was disappointed or relieved.

"Last night's break-in hasn't kept you down for long, has it?"

How she wished that were true! "I guess I recover quickly," she hedged, adding, "In a way it was a useful experience. I'll be ready the next time something happens." She looked up at his harshly planed face. "I won't let you down, Moss," she promised. "I'm really very good at my job. I'd love another chance to prove it."

"I can see that." His mouth curved into a semblance of a smile.

He was still worrying about her, Kat realized with a surge of tenderness, but he'd soon get over that. Just as she'd get over this urge to crawl into a safe, dark hole. Once she was working on the case again, everything would sort itself out. She'd regain her confidence, and she'd show Moss once and for all that he had nothing to fear on her account. She really *was* a good investigator—thorough, careful, and reasonably imaginative, with an instinctive knack for knowing which leads to follow and which to ignore.

Kat wiped her fingers on the napkin Moss had provided. "Are you going to tell Mark?" she asked, her mind turning over which leads she'd tackle first.

"Mark is the least of my worries at the moment."

Kat caught the repressive tone in his deep voice and stifled a small sigh of exasperation as she folded her arms behind her head. "You're already sorry you asked me to help, aren't you?"

"I haven't decided yet." Moss reached out, and with a light touch of his right forefinger, traced the small, jagged scar running down her exposed forearm. "You want to tell me how you got this?"

Kat lowered her arms. "That," she said succinctly, "is a souvenir from my checkered past."

"An accident?" Moss guessed.

"Not exactly." Kat hesitated. She'd never talked about it except with Ken, and then very briefly. She wasn't at all sure she wanted to see the expression on Moss's face if she told him now.

She pleated the sheet with her fingers, unable to decide. Finally she looked up, met the question in Moss's gray eyes, and said flatly, "It happened about two years ago. During a job."

"Kat, you don't have to—"

"Yes." She nodded once, decisively. "I do. I want to." She took a deep breath and plunged in. "It was while I was still apprenticing. We—Sam Blankenship and I—had been working on a child custody case. Actually," she amended, "we were trying to dig up dirt on the wife. It was a particularly nasty divorce, and the husband apparently wanted to get even by taking the kids. You know how it is."

Moss nodded. "I've suffered my share of those. Go on."

He refilled her coffee cup and handed it back.

Kat cradled it with both hands. "I was still fuzzy on all the details, so one night I decided to go back to the office after dinner. Sam had just recently come to trust me enough to give me a key." She smiled faintly, remembering the gruff bear of a man she'd apprenticed under. "So I let myself in . . . and inadvertently walked straight into a burglary in progress."

Kat took a long sip of hot coffee and carefully resettled the cup in her lap. Moss remained silent. "It wouldn't have been so bad if Derek and I hadn't just had one of our interminable fights," she continued slowly. "He'd just finished listing all the reasons I shouldn't be a private investigator—something he did on an average of once a week—and I was mad because I'd already quit my karate lessons to placate him. Being a private eye was bad enough, in his view, but being a karate expert was simply unacceptable. He figured women didn't need to know how to defend themselves; their men were supposed to do that for them. So "—Kat let a long, painful breath—"I walked into that office mad as hell and ready to do battle."

"You confronted the burglar," Moss ventured.

"Heck no. I *attacked* him." Kat smiled tightly. "And he didn't take too kindly to it. I'd had about six self-defense lessons before I quit. I knew just enough karate to get myself into deep trouble. Which I promptly did."

Moss considered her. "It was bad," he said quietly.

"I was beaten to within an inch of my life," said Kat in a rusty-sounding voice. She looked down and studied her hands. "The doctor tallied up two broken arms, one broken leg, a fractured jaw, three cracked ribs, a smashed collarbone, a concussion, and internal injuries too numerous to mention. I was in the hospital a very long time."

She took a deep breath and contemplated a crack in the ceiling. "You know, it's funny. Adversity is supposed to draw people together. At least that's what I'd always heard. Somehow, lying in the hospital all that time, I came to the conclusion that after what had happened, Derek would finally understand why I needed to know how to defend myself and give me his support. He didn't, naturally. He assumed

I'd learned my lesson. He figured that after the beating I'd taken, I'd come to my senses and abandon my silly notions about becoming a private eye."

"Instead, you took up karate again." Moss took the empty cup from her hands and set it on the tray.

"With a vengeance," Kat agreed grimly. "I vowed I'd never be helpless again. As soon as the doctor gave me the okay, I signed up for lessons. Derek filed for divorce less than a week later. And that," she finished with a bright, utterly insincere smile, "is the story of my life. Your turn."

"You want me to tell you how I was bested by a ninety-year-old woman with a baseball bat?"

"Is it true?" Kat tried to figure out the enigmatic expression on his face. "Or manufactured to make me feel better?"

"Honey," he purred, pulling the sheet from around her in one smooth move and tumbling her back across the bed, "I can think of more exciting ways than that to make you feel better." And with a deliciously wicked smile, hotly seeking lips, and both hands cupping the satin-smooth curves of her breasts, he proceeded to demonstrate them.

Afterward, they agreed to pool their information on the case.

"I'm not sure yet who's doing these crazy things or why," Kat conceded as they "helped" each other dress, "but there's got to be more here than meets the eye. I mean, who could possibly benefit when a model freaks out because someone slipped epoxy into her hair-setting lotion? It only delays a shoot until Mark's sorted things out. I've got a hunch— Will you please hold still?"

"I can't help it. That tickles. Here, let me help you with your bra. Turn around." Moss put his hands on her waist.

Kat removed them. "I don't trust you enough to turn my back on you. Where the dickens did you throw your underwear?"

"Never mind my underwear. Let's discuss yours. In fact, let's make this a hands-on discussion." His hands returned, sliding downward until his fingers curved around her bared bottom.

"Moss! You're supposed to be helping me think."

"I thought I was."

"Yes, but about the wrong thing. Will you please stop that? I'm trying to get into my panties."

"So am I."

Kat groaned. "A comedian. At this time of the morning, yet. Are you interested in hearing what I've found out or not?"

"I'm listening."

"You're doing a lot more than listening! Hold your hands up where I can keep an eye on them. Now, pick up your right foot. I can't tell the back from the front on these blasted briefs of yours." She tugged the black shorts up his tanned legs. "There." She playfully snapped the elastic waistband. "I'm finally beginning to feel safe. I think I may have discovered how they keep getting into the studio."

"How?" Moss reached around her back and unhooked her bra.

Kat rehooked it. "The skylight." She handed him his black jeans and reached for hers.

Moss held them out of reach. "The skylight is stuck shut."

Kat snatched her jeans and stepped into them. "One is. The other isn't. Are you going to help me zip my pants or not?"

"Patience, sweetheart. These things take time. No one could get in through either skylight. The only way up to the roof is by the rose trellis, and it's too weak to hold anyone up."

"No, it's not. I did it."

"Let me rephrase that. No sane person would attempt it."

"Thanks a lot! For your information—" Kat stopped. "Wait a minute. Dammit, I know that expression. You've already eliminated the skylight, haven't you?"

Moss smiled at her.

Kat disgustedly zipped up her jeans. "So much for my brilliant investigation. I was wondering why you hadn't done anything about it if that was how they were getting in. I suppose you deliberately left the skylight the way it was, hoping to catch the culprit. Which means, I suppose, you've set up some sort of surveillance. What was it, hidden cameras?"

"Would it upset you very much to know your escapade has been permanently captured on infrared film?"

"Don't say anything else or I may do something extremely uncivilized," Kat warned. "Have you seen my—never mind, there it is." She slipped her watch on. "Okay, so it's not the skylight. That leaves either the windows or the doors, both of which are locked at night."

"But not during the day."

Kat looked up from her search for a sweater. "You think this is all going on in broad daylight?" She blinked at him. "But wouldn't Mark have seen them, then?"

"As you may have noticed, Mark isn't the most observant person in the world. Tell me why you think he's not the real target." Moss zipped himself into his jeans and began buckling his belt.

"Because if someone is trying to ruin him, they're doing a terrible job of it. But mostly because he doesn't seem to have an enemy in the world. Not professionally, and not personally—" She stopped suddenly. "Cripes. A terrible thought just occurred to me. What if Mark *is* the target? What if the fires were *supposed* to do real damage but didn't because what we're dealing with is a bunglar? Someone not too bright?"

Moss said dryly, "Well, that takes in about ninety-nine percent of the women Mark's ever dated."

Kat thought for a moment, then shook her head. "No, it can't be one of them. Even his ex–girl friends—and that category seems to take in half the female population of San Francisco—have nothing but nice things to say about him. I can't see one of them trying to harm him."

"Mark's definitely got a way with women," Moss agreed.

"I'm glad you don't."

"Thank you, sweetheart. I love you, too."

Kat refrained from stamping her foot. "I didn't mean it that way, and you know it! I meant—oh, hell. You know what I meant."

Moss gathered her into his arms. "I do. And you don't ever need to worry on that score, Kat. I'm definitely a one-woman man." He kissed the top of her head. "And you're that woman."

Sighing, Kat snuggled up against his bare chest. "You're a terrible distraction. I've forgotten what I was talking about."

"You were saying something about Mark's way with women." Smiling blandly, Moss set her aside and pulled on his black turtleneck.

Wrinkling her nose at him, Kat picked up her own sweater. "Before you insisted on proving you could do this alone, I made up a list of all the things that have occurred at the studio and divided it into what happened to Mark's secretaries and what happened to his models and when. Then I made up another list of all the things that were missing and when they disappeared. Guess what?"

"There's a connection?" Moss reached for her sweater.

Kat quickly tugged it on. "Not with the secretaries," she conceded, fluffing out her hair. "I haven't the foggiest idea why they're being picked on. But every time something weird happens at one of Mark's photo sessions, something turns up missing. I immediately jumped to the conclusion that the motive was theft."

"That sounds promising."

Kat sat on the bed and slipped on her shoes. "My thoughts exactly. There's only one problem. The things that turn up missing aren't always valuable. In fact, sometimes they're ridiculously void of value. Carol Parker's tiger tooth lucky charm, for instance. Where's the motive in someone taking *that*? Another thing, if the motive is theft, why hasn't Mark's Hasselblad gone out the door? Some of his less expensive equipment has." Kat walked with Moss through the living room. "This is, without a doubt, the craziest case I've ever worked on. No motive, and no one is a suspect."

"It's a puzzler, all right, but you've gotten a long way in a short time." Moss locked the apartment door behind them and handed Kat her keys. "You're an amazing woman. Sexy as hell in that outfit, too."

Kat glanced down at her snug jeans and oversized navy

sweater. "Thank you, sir. Now, what have you found out so far?"

"I'll tell you in the car."

The problem was, Kat realized with growing exasperation, was that he didn't. Oh, he was cagey about it. But every time she brought up the subject, he managed to change it. As the minutes passed, her suspicions grew. Finally she turned and faced him.

"Moss Adams," she said warningly, "don't you dare back out on me. A deal is a deal. I told you everything I know about the case and—"

"Everything?"

"Yes, everything!" Kat fumed. "So stop stalling." She took a deep breath, trying to cool down, before going on more calmly, "I realize you're not used to having a partner. I realize, too," she added, trying to be understanding, "that it must be difficult for you, but—"

"Are you patronizing me?" Moss asked with interest.

"I'm going to murder you in a minute," Kat swore, "if you don't—Where are you taking me?" she asked suddenly.

"Police headquarters." Moss shot her a bland smile.

Kat eyed him suspiciously. "What for?"

"To see the Armenian Connection."

"The Armenian Connection?" Kat echoed blankly, massaging the lingering soreness in her left shoulder.

"Yan Bagdasarian. A friend I have in the department." Moss neatly pulled the Corvette into an empty parking slot. Shutting off the engine, he turned toward her, dropping one arm along the back of her seat. "I thought it might be a good idea if we checked over the petty larceny files to see if anybody besides Mark is having similiar problems with thefts combined with sabotage."

Eyebrows raised, Kat queried, "You think this all might be some sort of modus operandi that has nothing to do with Mark?" That angle had never even occured to her. She must be slipping, she decided.

Moss shrugged. "Who knows?" He lifted a strand of her thick russet hair and began winding it around his forefinger while Kat did her best to breathe. "It might be worth checking out. What do you say we get on with it?" He tugged the lock of hair lightly. "It might take a while."

A frisson of awareness shimmied up Kat's spine at the familiar, affectionate gesture. "We're both going to work on it?" she managed breathlessly.

One tawny eyebrow rose. "I thought you said you wanted to work with me on the case. I could do this alone if you've changed your mind . . ."

"No! No." Kat bit her lip in consternation. "I didn't mean that. It just seems, well, inefficient to have us both doing the same thing. I mean, I'm sure they have everything in a computer. One of us ought to be working on some other angle, don't you think?" It was crazy, but somehow she didn't want to seem pushy on the issue. A female partner for a man who didn't like partners in the first place was one thing. An aggressive female partner was probably something else again.

Moss tapped his free hand on the steering wheel. "You may be right," he conceded after a moment. "What do you suggest we do?"

Kat was never sure later why she insisted on being the one to check the police files while Moss went off to other, probably more interesting, tasks. Partly, she suspected, because she knew he wanted to skip over to his house to change his clothes. And partly because he seemed determined not to push the clerical—some might say feminine—duties on her. She felt obligated to reassure him that she really didn't mind drudge work. It was, after all, part of any job. This was her golden opportunity, her chance to show Moss just what kind of stuff she was made of. And she didn't want to blow it by seeming to disdain the often tedious, frequently boring, albeit necessary research that most cases required.

Two hours later, however, she wasn't feeling quite so generous. Kat scanned the files mounded on the table in front of her with a jaundiced eye. It was going to take her days and days—no, weeks and weeks, possibly forever—to wade her way through the tons of paperwork.

"There must be an easier way!" she muttered. And, of course, there was. Except the computer was down that morning, and Yan Bagdasarian had already dolefully assured her it would be out of commission for some time.

"You look bushed. Maybe this will help." The petite brunette who worked under Bagdasarian set down a cup of coffee at Kat's elbow. "Bad luck your picking today to do that," she commented with a commiserating shake of her head.

"You're telling me." Kat gave a twisted smile and thanked the other woman for the coffee.

The brunette waved her hand in dismissal. "Don't mention it. It's the least I can do for a fellow girl Friday. You know," she added thoughtfully, "you ought to get in touch with that blond guy who was in last week looking up the same files."

Kat's coffee cup stopped halfway to her mouth. "Blond guy?" she repeated, her smile suddenly pasted to her face.

"A friend of Yan's. I think his name was Mace," the brunette mused, "or Marsh, or something unusual like that. Big, blond, and beautiful. Almost made me wish I weren't married. He had me run off a copy of all that stuff, breaking everything down by location and what not. If you need the same information, you might try calling him up and asking if you can take a peek."

"I just might do that," Kat muttered, closing the file before her with a small bang. She also might strangle him!

That man! She knew exactly what he was doing now, and she was furious! Talk about tricky, he'd actually gotten her to *insist* on looking up the police files. Of all the sneaky, conniving ways to keep her out of harm's way, planting her squarely inside the police department was surely the most inventive. And to think she'd actually believe he wanted—no, needed—her help. What that man *really* needed, she decided, was a lesson.

Kat looked up from her clenched fists and saw a chagrined-looking Yan Bagdasarian making what appeared to be a hurried phone call. To Moss? Picking up her small purse, Kat slung it over her shoulder and walked briskly out of the building, determined to show Moss Adams once and for all that it wasn't nice to fool Mother Nature. Or one's own partner. Especially one's *female* partner.

She who laughs last, Kat thought in grim satisfaction as she climbed into a taxi, laughs best.

CHAPTER

Thirteen

IT WAS NEARLY five the next morning when Kat let herself back into her apartment. Yawning, she dropped her purse onto the hall table—which served as a general depository for mail, newspapers, and anything else she left there and promptly forgot—and unbuttoned her suede jacket. Hanging it behind the door, she made her way in the dark toward her bedroom. All in all, she decided, suppressing another yawn, it had been one hell of a day. Not bothering to turn on a light—she was going to fall into bed in less than thirty seconds anyway, she reasoned—she toed her low-heeled shoes off her aching feet and was in the process of tugging off her sweater when the lamp next to her bed flicked on.

Gasping, Kat spun around and automatically threw her hands up in a position of self-defense as her eyes adjusted to the light. Her gaze settled on the large masculine form taking up half her unmade bed, and a sigh of relief, mingled with a new kind of apprehension, escaped her lips.

"Moss!" she croaked. She lowered her arms to her sides and, with instinctive wariness, surveyed the unshaven face of the man stretched out on the eyelet-edged sheets. "How did you get in here?"

"My American Express card," he answered laconically. "Like Karl Malden, I never leave home without it." Gray eyes shadowed from obvious lack of sleep gave her a slow, thorough appraisal. "You mind telling me just where the hell you've been?" Even though his deep voice sounded only mildly reproving, Kat could have sworn a sizable amount of male menace filled the tiny bedroom.

Propped up against the wall for support now that her knees had unaccountably started to wobble, she lifted her chin in defiance and replied sweetly, "Out." Then she added in dulcet tones that shouldn't have fooled a four-year-old, "Working."

"On the case?" Again Moss's voice was calm. In a more imaginative mood Kat might have called it dangerously quiet.

"That's right." She took in his wrinkled brown shirt and equally creased tan slacks and wondered what he'd been up to. "Got any objections?"

"Would it matter to you if I did?" came the soft reply.

If he had yelled or threatened or stomped around the room in a fit of machismo anger, Kat could have responded with enough matching anger to fuse glass. But somehow his steady composure took the wind out of her sails. Damn the man, she reflected irritably. Why couldn't he be *predictable?* Making sure she was safely out of reach, she tentatively reached down and began massaging her sore feet and considered the inadvisability of trying to put in a full day's work the day after being battered by doors, floors, and other inanimate objects.

"You look like you've had a long day," Moss noted neutrally.

"I have," Kat assured him, stretching. "A very long day. A very interesting one, too," she added with a goading little smile.

Retribution gleamed in Moss's gray eyes. "Tell me about it."

"I'm sure you don't want to hear all the boring details," Kat demurred.

"Bore me," Moss urged, looking faintly homicidal.

But after Kat had related only a fraction of her day's activities, skimming over her visit downtown to see Manny Manetti,a reputed crime figure, Moss was beginning to look appalled. Or was it horrified?

"What the hell were you doing down there?" Moss demanded, looking as if he was having trouble keeping his hands off her.

"I thought he might know something," Kat retorted, arching her sore back.

"He knows a lot of things," Moss growled back. "None of which *you* ought to get yourself involved in. My God, woman, if I'd known where you'd actually *been,* instead of where I imagined you'd be, I would've called out a SWAT team!"

Kat raised her hands in exasperation. "Damn you, don't you dare try to make me the guilty party! If anyone ought to be feeling guilty around here," she told him, trying to sound forceful but managing to sound simply what she was— dead tired, "it's you."

Her eyes clashed with his for a moment. To her surprise, his dropped away first to catalogue the signs of exhaustion on her face.

"Why didn't you call?" The pain evident in the stark question surprised Kat.

"Why didn't you tell the truth?" she countered, praying her legs would continue to hold her up and not drop her ignobly to the floor.

"I was worried about you. Come sit down before you fall down." He patted the spot on the bed next to him.

Kat shook her head. "I don't think I can walk that far. Besides, I don't trust you. You might have something violent in mind, and I like my neck exactly the way it is."

"You're admitting I might have cause for violence, then?"

"I'm not admitting anything of the sort," Kat retorted aloofly.

Again Moss studied her. "You know what you are?"

"A wronged woman?" Kat guessed.

"An argumentative woman. I'll bet if I told you the earth

was round, you'd insist it was square just to goad me."

"Don't be silly." Kat gave him a disparaging look. "Everyone knows the earth is flat."

Moss smiled then, very slowly, and rose leisurely from the bed.

"Touch me," Kat swore shakily, as he began walking toward her, "and I'll...I'll..."

Moss touched her. In fact, he caught her as she started to move away from him and promptly began sliding to the carpeted floor.

"Moss!"

Ignoring her protesting wail, he lifted her effortlessly into his arms and carried her to the bed, where he propped her up against a bank of pillows. Kat sighed and peered cautiously up at him.

"Are you terribly mad at me?"

"I haven't decided yet." Moss sat down on the bed next to her and examined her face. "When did you last eat?"

Kat couldn't remember.

Shaking his blond head and muttering something about pigheaded women, Moss left the room and reappeared approximately ten minutes later. He held the plate of scrambled eggs under Kat's nose until the heavenly smell slowly opened her closed eyes.

"Don't go to sleep on me yet," he scolded, gently tucking a napkin under her chin. "You and I still have some talking to do."

"Oh?" Kat sat up, more lethargic than wary. "About what?"

But Moss refused to talk further until she'd finished the delectably fluffy eggs, polished off a small bowl of fruit cocktail, and demolished two toasted bagels.

Refilling her mug with decaffeinated coffee, he took the empty plate off her lap, noting, "Nothing wrong with your appetite, I see."

Kat shrugged. "You're a better cook than I am."

Moss raised an eyebrow. "Trying to soften me up?"

"Is it working?" Kat stifled a yawn.

"Not so you'd notice. I'm tempted to ask how you happen

to know Manny Manetti, but I won't. Tell me what else you've been up to today."

Kat set her cup on her lap. "Why?"

"Because if you don't," Moss replied amiably, "I might change my mind and decide to strangle you."

"Oh, well." Kat yawned again. "If that's the way you're going to be . . . I was at Frank Morgan's apartment. Among other interesting places," she couldn't help adding.

Moss closed his eyes momentarily. "I'm sure I'm going to regret asking. Doing what?"

Kat smiled and cooed, "Looking for evidence, of course."

Moss's left eyebrow rose a fraction. "He didn't mind your nosing around?"

"That's hard to say," Kat confided. "He wasn't there for me to ask."

"Then how did you get in?" Moss asked pleasantly.

Kat feigned innocence. "With my VISA card, naturally, since, unlike you, I don't have an American Express. I always knew that thing would be useful for something besides undermining my finances," she added in satisfaction.

"You do realize, I hope, that what you did was illegal."

"I didn't steal anything," Kat protested.

"Good. *That*," Moss pointed out sternly, "is called larceny."

"Desperate situations call for desperate measures," said Kat self-righteously.

"Tell that to the police."

Kat opened her mouth to argue, then stopped. "Oh, all right," she relented, "I know it was wrong. I have just as strong a code of ethics as you do, but that man is involved in all of this, I just know it."

"How do you know it?"

"Instinct. He's the only person I know of who isn't totally charmed by Mark."

"That isn't exactly a compelling reason to launch an attack on Mark's studio," Moss noted.

"No," Kat agreed, "but greed combined with opportunity has a nasty way of getting out of hand. Mark, naive soul that he is, simply provided the perfect setup. Did you realize

Frank Morgan was present when three of the fires at Mark's studio broke out, including the one during which Darcy Meadows's diamond watch disappeared? Did you also know," Kat continued, warming to her subject, "that he was once picked up on suspicion of arson but was let go due to lack of evidence? Ah, you didn't know that?" Kat batted her eyes in satisfaction at having at least one piece of information Moss didn't. "Well, he was. And if that isn't incriminating enough, how about the fact that at least two-thirds of the models who've had trouble at Mark's studio were from his agency? He's the only one I can think of who knew enough about those shoots ahead of time to booby-trap all the props. Every bone in my body tells me he's responsible for what's going on."

"You're saying the motive behind all this is theft, and Morgan's the culprit?" Moss settled himself on the bed and pulled her close.

Kat sighed against his shoulder. "Well, jewelry and watches are fairly easy to fence. So is camera equipment. His models say Morgan's greedy. Maybe he decided to augment his income the easy way. Goodness knows, stealing beats hard work any day of the week."

"I'm going to assume that theory is your way of explaining the thefts and doesn't reflect your personal philosophy of life. What about the other things, like the shoes and bras disappearing? Did his models tell you if Morgan has any strange fetishes?"

Kat wrinkled her nose at him. "Don't be snide. If you hadn't scared Mark's ex-secretaries half to death, then grilled all the models like Torquemada, they would've confided in you, too. I think the missing Guccis and Maidenforms were probably just a distraction."

"I thought I'd been positively charming with Kim Lambertson."

"Darling, insinuating a woman's overweight condition is the reason her desk chair dissolved beneath her is not what I'd call being charming."

"Hmm. You may be right. Speaking of Mark's secretaries, why all the accidents involving them? The shorted-out typewriter could have been another potential arson attempt gone awry—"

Kat nodded. "Like the frayed cord on the coffeepot."

"—but why the dissolving chairs and falling ceiling tiles?"

"Distraction again?" Kat guessed. "The same reason things like the fake smoke machine emitting tear gas keep happening. It makes it a lot easier to swipe something like Emma Li's jade ring when people are running around like headless chickens. And wreaking havoc on the secretaries until they quit not only added to the chaos; it had the additional benefit of eliminating any continuity in the office, so no one was likely to make a connection between the events. It was a pretty sure bet Mark wouldn't," she added apologetically.

"Mark isn't known for his brains," Moss agreed easily. He reached up and gently pushed her hair away from her face. "So you think all the sabotage was intended to muddle things?"

Yawning, Kat shrugged. "It pretty effectively clouded the real issue—the thefts—which in turn made the motive harder to pinpoint. The trouble is"—she frowned—"none of the stolen jewelry or camera gear is at his place. And none of it seems to have resurfaced, which means Morgan hasn't tried to fence it yet. At least not locally. That's what I wanted to ask Manny Manetti about. In any case, his bank account hasn't swelled appreciably, so he probably hasn't managed to sell it. And he hasn't gotten into his safe deposit box recently, either. I checked that. So he can't have stashed it."

"Maybe he rented another safe deposit box somewhere?" Moss suggested in a tone that had Kat wondering just how much he already knew of what she was telling him. And whether he'd gotten hold of the supposedly confidential bank information the same way she had.

She shook her head. "I don't think so. I've contacted more banks than you can shake a stick at."

"Or opened a new bank account?"

"No. I checked that, too."

"Or rented a locker at the airport? Or possibly the bus depot?"

"Nope. Ever since that bomb scare they've been watching both those areas like hawks. I flashed Morgan's picture around to the security guards, and no one remembers seeing him at either place."

"My," said Moss mildly, "you *have* been busy, haven't you?"

"Have you?" Kat retorted. "Been busy, I mean." She eyed him in challenge. "You know, you still haven't told me what you know. I suppose you eliminated Frank Morgan as a suspect the first day, and I've simply been wasting my time."

"Not exactly. My instincts tell me he's involved in some way, too. But instinct doesn't hold up very well in court. Evidence does. Having him at TJ's the last time a model lost something of value puts him close to the scene of the crime, but not, I'm afraid, close enough."

Kat bit her lower lip. "Who says he was at TJ's?"

"Seven people, including Jake, the owner."

"Damn. It can't have been Frank, then. Unless he's a lot smarter than he looks and has figured out how to be in two places at once."

"No," Moss agreed, looking thoughtful. "It couldn't, could it?"

"On the other hand, he might have an accomplice. Maybe I could try confronting him," Kat suggested. "He might incriminate himself."

"Or maybe," said Moss with a quelling look, "he'll do something desperate."

"I'm not afraid of him!" said Kat indignantly.

"I know," Moss muttered. "That's what worries me. We confront him together, as a team. Or not at all."

"Where are we going?" Kat asked in his car fifteen minutes later. Moss had given her time for a ten-second shower, thrown a small armful of clean clothes into the bathroom when she'd finished, awakened her when she started to fall asleep standing up—both times—and then bundled her into the Corvette before she had a chance to nod off again. Kat had slumped down in the bucket seat before he could start the engine.

"Are you going to fall asleep on me again?" he asked, guiding the Corvette smoothly into the early morning traffic.

"That depends," said Kat, trying to keep her eyes open, "on where we're going. Frank Morgan lives the other way."

"I know. We're going to go see a friend of mine first."

"A bit early, don't you think, for social calls?"

"This friend keeps early hours," explained Moss.

The green belt of Golden Gate Park passed by Kat's window. Lord, she was tired. Too tired to argue, too tired to protest, too tired to confront anyone at the moment, including Moss.

She rolled her head to the left and studied his profile. His hair was ruffled by the cool ocean breeze slipping through the car's open windows, but despite the fact that he'd obviously been up all night worrying about her, he didn't look half as bedraggled as she felt.

In fact, Kat decided, despite his wrinkled clothes and unshaven face, he looked calm and collected and in full control of himself and the situation.

In fact, she realized with a sudden quiver of alarm, he was looking decidedly pleased with himself. It wasn't until they were halfway across the Golden Gate Bridge that Kat figured out why.

She was being kidnapped.

CHAPTER

Fourteen

KAT SAT UP and stared at him, unwilling at first to believe it was happening. Then he turned his head slightly, sliding her a brief, questioning glance, and she knew. Beyond any doubt, she knew.

"You tricked me again!" she breathed, appalled at how trusting she'd been yet a second time. When was she ever going to learn? she wondered in thorough self-disgust. The man was demonstrably unpredictable, infinitely unscrupulous, plainly willing to do anything it took to get what he wanted. Never mind that he said he loved her. She loved him, too, but that wasn't the issue. He was patronizing her again, treating her like a child—and a not very bright one at that.

"You never had any intention of letting me work with you on this case," she accused, "did you?"

Moss didn't even blink. "Nope."

Kat suppressed the urge to throttle him. "Then why pretend you were? Why pretend we were going to confront Frank Morgan together?"

"You're a very determined woman. I had to do something

to keep you from killing yourself. After you caught on to me before, this seemed as good a way as any."

He wasn't even bothering to deny it, Kat realized. And why should he? It was as plain as day that she was helpless to do anything about it. She could hardly jump out of the Corvette when he was going sixty-plus miles an hour.

"How could you do such a thing?" she wailed.

"Because I don't want to see you get hurt."

The calm assumption she still needed protecting and his infuriating certainty he was doing the right thing aggravated Kat until all she could do was sputter, "Oh, you . . . you . . . arrogant . . . overbearing . . . condescending . . ."

"Careful," he warned, "you'll get high blood pressure bottling up your feelings like this."

"Don't you dare laugh at me, you . . . you . . ." Why couldn't she think of anything appropriate to call him? Kat wondered in exasperation. Because the man defied description!

"Let me out of this car this instant," she fumed, "or I swear I'll have you arrested!"

"For what?" Moss asked with maddening calm, maneuvering the black Corvette through heavy bridge traffic.

"For what?" Kat looked at him in open disbelief. "For kidnapping me! In case you haven't heard, kidnapping is a federal crime!"

"I'm not kidnapping you—"

"Then let me out of this car!"

"—I'm putting you in protective custody."

Kat felt as if she were talking to a brick wall. He could be every bit as stubborn as she could when he set his mind to it, and every bit as unreasonable.

"You're unbelievable," she concluded, shaking her head in wonder. "You're really going to kidnap me for my own good? To keep me out of trouble?"

"It seems the logical thing to do," he acknowledged.

Logical! Kat rolled her eyes toward heaven.

"You mind telling me where you're taking me?" They were driving off the Golden Gate Bridge now, heading north.

"My cabin in the Sierras," Moss answered readily, apparently deciding there was nothing she could do about it even if she wanted to.

Kat definitely wanted to. She had absolutely no intention of being kidnapped or put into protective custody or whatever Moss cared to call it.

"Why don't you sit back and relax?" Moss suggested soothingly, downshifting for a turn. "It'll take us a couple of hours to get there."

Sliding down into the buttery-soft leather seat, Kat yawned, plotting despite her weariness. Moss didn't realize it, but she could be as sneaky as he could. With that pleasant thought in mind, she finally gave in to her body's demands and dozed off.

She awoke about two hours later as the Corvette slowed down. When she realized where they were, some of her original optimism died on the spot. Moss had turned off the main highway, and they were heading down a dirt road of dubious negotiability. Throat-clogging dust clouded the air as the Corvette steadily climbed a rutted path that looked far more receptive to goats than to anything automotive.

When Moss finally stopped the car, Kat could only stare glumly ahead, her last hopes of freedom dashed. They were out in the middle of nowhere, miles from anything even approaching civilization.

"Here we are," Moss said, sounding disgustingly cheery.

Kat eyed first him and then the building before them. "What, pray tell, is *that?*"

"My summer cabin," Moss explained helpfully.

"Cabin? That's something of an exaggeration, isn't it? Surely you mean shack."

Moss simply smiled at the caustic observation. "It needs a little repair, is all. Once it gets a new roof and a new floor and a new porch——" He stopped when he caught Kat's expression, then continued almost apologetically, "It's really not bad inside——"

"——for a prison," Kat finished for him with a cloying smile.

Moss took her hand. "Cheer up, honey. We'll be alone, in a beautiful setting. We can make love from dawn to dusk if you like—"

"I don't like."

"I thought you liked my company," he said in amused complaint, kissing her palm.

Kat snatched her hand back. "I *did*."

"I don't see why you're so determined to be angry."

"That," said Kat repressively, "is because you're arrogant, high-handed, and overbearing. How would you feel if the situation were reversed?"

"Flattered," Moss responded. When Kat let out a snort of disbelief, he explained, "I'd be flattered that you cared enough to want to keep me out of harm's way."

"If that's a plea for peace, you can just forget it."

Moss sighed. "Something tells me," he predicted with a rueful shake of his tawny head, "that this is going to be a very interesting experience for both of us. Come on inside, honey, and let's get settled. Then we'll talk."

Unmollified by his conciliatory tone, Kat followed him into the cabin. Moss stood in the little kitchenette, unloading food from the small ice chest he'd extracted from the back of his car.

"I bought you some yogurt," he said, putting an assortment of cartons and packages into the tiny refrigerator. "With only a gas-run generator for power, I can't store too many cold things. But if there's anything else you're crazy about, let me know and I'll try South Shore tomorrow."

Kat's left eyebrow had slowly been rising as he spoke until it now arched ominously. "What makes you think I like yogurt?"

"Ken told me." He turned and delivered an impossibly innocent smile. "Didn't I tell you? I talked with him on the phone this morning while you were sleeping in the shower. Your brother's very reasonable, isn't he? Not like you at all."

"I don't have a brother," Kat declared. "I just disowned him. Did you tell him you were planning to kidnap me?"

"Yep."

Undercover Kisses

"And?"

"When I told him why, he was all for it. He knows how stubborn you can be when you think you're right."

"I don't think I'm right," Kat fumed as another source of potential rescue disappeared before her eyes. "I know I am!"

Moss smiled blandly and continued to unpack the groceries. Eyeing him balefully, Kat wandered over to the large stone fireplace, which had been set with kindling and two logs, ready to be lit.

"It gets cold here at night, even in summer," Moss commented.

"It's going to be downright frigid in here tonight," Kat promised. Ignoring Moss's smile of denial, she dropped herself onto the leather sofa and contemplated her surroundings. Despite the state of disrepair outside, the interior wasn't half-bad, she decided. Though sparsely furnished, it was cozy in a rustic sort of way, with natural wood paneling and a woven grass floor mat. Other than the couch, a round wooden table and two chairs of questionable vintage, plus a low dresser painted an unfortunate shade of green, graced the room. But it had potential. In fact, with a good sweeping out and a little sprucing up it might even be habitable, she conceded.

Suddenly wary, Kat sat up and eyed Moss. "You know, if you have any ideas about turning me into chief cook and bottle washer or any kind of housekeeper," she warned, "forget it. I'm a prisoner who doesn't believe in hard labor."

"Don't worry," Moss said peaceably, placing boxes in the knotty-pine cabinets. "We'll share the domestic duties. I'll even cook the steaks tonight. You can have your turn in the kitchen tomorrow."

That wasn't what she wanted to hear! "Just how long are you going to keep me here?" she demanded, getting up and stalking to the butcher-block counter.

"As long as it takes," he answered cryptically. "How many sandwiches would you like? One or two?"

They ate lunch in silence, but it was anything but companionable. Finally Kat couldn't stand it anymore. She threw

down her napkin in disgust and glared at him. "I still can't
believe you're doing this. Here we are, tucked away in the
middle of nowhere, when we ought to be in San Francisco
working on the case."

"There's no need to get so excited," Moss said, calmly
finishing his sandwich. "The case is solved. You solved it."

Kat stared at him. "*I* solved it?" she repeated blankly.
When Moss nodded slowly, she asked with just a touch of
sarcasm, "Well, would you mind enlightening me, then?
Tell me how I did it, and then tell me who 'dun' it."

Moss reached over the table and tweaked her left earlobe.
"You did it as any good private eye does: through elimi-
nation. And the ones who 'dun' it are Laurel Tandy and
Candy-Anna Carpenter."

Kat blinked twice, absently touching the spot Moss had
lightly pinched. Laurel Tandy and Candy-Anna Carpenter.
Laurel Tandy and Candy-Anna Carpenter? Laurel Tandy and
Candy-Anna Carpenter!

"With the assistance of Emma Li, another of Frank Morgan's models," Moss added.

Kat watched him with a feeling of unreality. Up until
now it had never occurred to her that *any* of the models
might be responsible, let alone three of them. "How do you
figure *I* solved the case?" she asked. "I was convinced Frank
Morgan was involved."

"He *is* involved. He was the target." Moss ran a forefinger over her cheek. "And you solved the case because it
was your observations that clicked everything into place."

"My observations?" said Kat, still blankly, a rush of
warmth surging through her capillaries at his touch.

Moss nodded, tracing her lower lip with his thumb. "You
were the one who figured out the sabotaged props were
providing distraction and that what was happening to the
secretaries was simply subterfuge. And you were the one
who figured out Mark wasn't the target, that he just provided
the perfect set of circumstances. You were also right about
the motive. It was theft. But only later on. Originally it was
revenge."

"Revenge?" Kat repeated, still feeling a little like Alice tumbling into Wonderland.

"Mark might not have any enemies," Moss explained, "but Frank Morgan does. Partly because, as you pointed out, he's greedy. And partly because he treats his models like so much meat at the market. Laurel Tandy and Candy-Anna Carpenter apparently got sick and tired of Morgan and his attitude and decided to do something about it."

"Like framing him for the arson attempts?" Kat guessed, liking the way their thinking meshed. "And discovering how easy it would be to steal a few baubles at the same time?"

"Once they found out he'd been picked up on similar charges, the temptation to set him up must have been ir-resistible."

"Wouldn't it have been easier if they'd just left his mod-eling agency?"

"Easier, but then, they would have missed out on all those 'baubles,' as you put it. Besides that, slow revenge is almost always more satisfying."

"They must really have been ticked off at him."

"They were," Moss agreed. "Even so, it got out of hand. But, as we all know, hell hath no fury like a woman who thinks she's being patronized."

Or one who's been kidnapped against her will? Kat won-dered, leaning back from Moss's distracting fingers. She contemplated the man before her. The man she loved. The man she could cheerfully strangle . . .

"Are you telling me," she inquired dangerously, "that you've kidnapped me to protect me from three light-fingered *models?*"

Moss looked like a man with his hand caught in the cookie jar. "These three aren't your average models. So far they've collectively demonstrated a remarkable talent for intimidation. Just ask some of Mark's former secretaries."

"I'm not afraid of them!" Kat denied forcefully.

"That," said Moss, "is the problem. And that, sweet lady, is why you're here. Until I'm sure you won't try any more dangerous stunts, I'm not taking any chances." He gave her a placating half smile. "Believe me, Kat, I understand your need to prove your competence as an investigator. I'm just afraid of losing you while you go about it."

Moss made a concerted effort to defuse the situation all afternoon, Kat conceded, as he set about airing out the cabin. Faintly disgusted with herself for caving in, she watched him work for about ten minutes, then pitched in. Grabbing a broom, she swept the floor and then washed down the kitchen counter and cabinets while Moss attacked the small bathroom. By the time they were done, the cabin was spotless and the sun was sinking below the horizon.

Moss insisted on grilling the steaks and making the salad, and then was equally adamant about cleaning up afterward. Not at all sure how she was going to remain angry at him when he was being so impossibly *nice,* Kat took her glass of California Pinot Noir over to the large leather sofa and sat down before the crackling fire.

"Where are the beds?" she asked curiously, scanning the cabin anew for hidden crevices. There were none.

"You're sitting on it."

The offhand way Moss said it pricked up her ears. "It?" she repeated ominously. When he smiled blandly and nodded, she pointedly asked, "Where are you going to sleep?"

Moss had refilled his own wineglass and perched on the arm of the couch. "Where do you think?" he chided.

"I'm not sleeping with you," Kat said firmly, "if that's what you have in mind."

But she did. She didn't really have a whole lot of choice, she admitted, unless she wanted to sleep on the floor. Moss plainly wasn't giving up his creature comforts to assuage her, and in a more reasonable mood she would have accepted that without batting an eyelash. Unfortunately, she wasn't in a particularly reasonable mood.

Refusing to undress, she lay on top of the covers fully clothed while Moss stripped down to his briefs. She tensed involuntarily, her heart thumping wildly as his hands went to the elastic waistband.

"Stop looking at me like that," he scolded wearily, keeping the briefs on as he climbed into the opened hide-a-bed.

"I'm not going to press myself on you. I haven't slept in over twenty-four hours. To tell you the truth, I'm too exhausted to be anything but a total gentleman."

Which made Kat feel bitchy and selfish and guilty as the very devil. It was because of her that he hadn't gotten any sleep the previous night. And, like her, he probably had all sorts of things he ought to be doing in the city. Instead, he was spending an indefinite amount of time holed up in the mountains. Because of her.

Moss sank down onto the firm mattress and immediately managed to push loose the bottom half of the blankets with his long legs. Groaning, he started to get up to tuck them back into place. Kat pushed him back down with one finger and went around to the foot of the bed to reanchor the bedding.

"What am I going to do with you?" she asked, shaking her head. No matter how she rearranged things, Moss's feet still overhung the end of the bed by at least eight inches.

"Come keep me warm while you decide," he suggested, hooking her waist with a long, tanned arm and lazily pulling her down on top of him. "These sheets are cold."

Half sprawled across him, able to feel every warm inch of his lean frame, Kat lifted her head and found Moss smiling contentedly, his eyes closed. An ache of longing so strong it hurt swept through her body. Unable to help herself, she reached up and brushed her knuckles lightly over the stubble of beard on his unshaven chin.

"You look like a desperado."

"Desperately tired is more like it. Kat?"

"Hmm?" Rolling off him, she lay next to him, her head cradled on his bare shoulder. She rubbed her nose across his collarbone, savoring his scent, the smooth satin texture of his skin.

"I'm sorry I had to kidnap you."

"I know." Kat swallowed the lump forming in her throat. An almost physical need to comfort him welled inside her. "Go to sleep."

He was silent for perhaps two minutes. Kat was almost certain he'd dozed off when he said drowsily, "Kat?"

"Hmm?"

"Are you still mad at me?"

"Furious. I'm thinking of strangling you in your sleep. If you ever go to sleep," she added in stern reprimand.

"You would, too." Moss smiled faintly. Another minute passed. "Kat?"

Kat sighed loudly. "Go to sleep," she scolded, mussing his soft hair. "You've had a long day. We both have. We'll talk tomorrow."

As his breathing deepened and it became increasingly evident he was finally falling asleep, Kat moved ever so slightly closer. Nestled against his warmth, she reached up and lightly smoothed back the hair from his hard-planed cheeks. Her fingertips tenderly traced the deep lines of weariness etched on his face. Another pang of remorse shot through her, followed swiftly by sadness.

"I love you, shortstuff," he murmured, pulling her still closer and kissing her forehead, his lips sweetly tender and lingering.

And I love you, Kat thought, wondering just how long she could keep up this pretense of anger at him. It was the only way she could think of to wedge some distance between them. And she *had* to separate herself from him, Kat knew. Mentally, and then physically. Because she knew, even if he didn't yet realize it, that they were never going to make it together.

It had been on her mind all day. She had alternately denied it and accepted it. But when push came to shove, she didn't think there was a chance in the world of their ever resolving the basic conflict between them: Moss's apparent need to protect her because of her so-called helplessness.

It was because she'd lost her head the night her apartment had been broken into, Kat admitted, that he still felt so strongly about it. He had no way of knowing that had been the exception rather than the rule. But if he ever fully realized just how unhelpless she really was, she knew exactly how he'd feel, and it wouldn't be protective. It would be a lot more like threatened . . .

Moss was dressed and drinking a cup of coffee when she woke the next morning. There was no moment of disorientation as she opened her eyes. She knew exactly where she was and with whom. And she knew today was the day she had to escape, for Moss's good as well as her own.

"Morning, sleepyhead. Rest okay?" In his navy T-shirt and jeans, Moss looked awake and refreshed and in decidedly good humor.

"You snore," Kat said, trying to work up some defensive anger at him. All she managed to feel was depressed.

"So do you," he replied easily. "Coffee?" When Kat nodded, he poured her a cupful, added cream and sugar just the way she liked it, and brought it over.

The *rightness* of waking up in the same room with him, the almost marital intimacy of having him bring her coffee as she sat in bed, formed a lump in Kat's throat so big it felt like a cantaloupe. Her eyes feasted on him, then dropped away. This man wasn't hers, she reminded herself grimly, and never would be. And the sooner she reconciled herself to that, the better.

"Are you going to be this grumpy all day?" he asked, sitting beside her on the sleep-rumpled bed.

Kat forced herself to swallow the coffee in her mouth. "I tend to get grumpy when I'm kidnapped," she said, refusing to look at him.

She felt Moss's eyes on her, but all he said was, "My culinary talents extend to making pancakes. Would you like some?"

"I'm not really hungry. You go ahead."

"I already ate. Two hours ago, in fact. You're a hard sleeper. I got the distinct impression I could have made love to you for the past couple of hours and you wouldn't have known a thing."

Kat looked up so abruptly she nearly spilled her coffee. "You didn't . . . ?"

Moss looked impossibly injured. "Would I take advantage of you like that?" he asked, then spoiled the effect by musing, "You look very sweet and innocent when you're sleeping. Like a little girl. Except for the black lacy underwear. Now *that's* all woman. By the way, your clothes are hanging over the chair behind you."

Kat felt the slow rise of heat in her cheeks as the fact that she was virtually nude beneath the covers sank into her still sleep-fogged brain.

"You undressed me while I was defenseless?" she yelped.

Moss raised his eyebrows. "Someone had to," he reasoned. "You were too stubborn to do it yourself last night. Besides that, it was a matter of self-defense. Your buttons kept digging into me. And since when were you ever defenseless?"

Kat quelled the sudden surge of hope leaping up inside her. It was a purely rhetorical question, she decided, not to be taken too seriously.

Moss was outside chopping firewood when she emerged from the cabin. Dressed in jeans and a Western-style shirt, she sat on the top step of the small porch and watched him for about an hour, her chin cupped in her palm and a look of patent boredom on her face whenever Moss glanced over at her.

In truth, Kat was anything but bored. Moss looked wonderfully, magnificently male. The well-toned muscles of his arms and neck gleamed with sweat as he raised and lowered the small ax, splitting the chunks of wood and stacking them neatly against the side of the cabin. Passing by her once, he winked as if he could read her mind. As if he knew how much she wanted him.

Cheeks flaming, Kat turned away, refusing to respond to the affectionate teasing. It was going to be hard enough to leave him without his reminding her of how very much she loved him. What would she do without him?

While Moss was in the shower, cooling off after his morning's task, Kat got her first opportunity to escape, and even then she had to force herself to take advantage of it. Waiting until he was well into an off-tune rendition of "Some Enchanted Evening," Kat reluctantly started rummaging in his jean pockets for his car keys. She wasn't sure if she felt triumphant or just plain disappointed when her fingers closed over the hard piece of metal. Shooting a long, lingering look at the closed bathroom door, she tiptoed out of the cabin and headed for the Corvette.

She was still sitting in the driver's seat, staring out the dusty windshield in fulminating irritation, when Moss, dressed in clean jeans and a fresh T-shirt, sauntered out and bent down beside the car.

"Going somewhere?" he inquired through the open window.

This time it was Kat who headed for the shower to cool off. Moss hadn't even bothered to deny sabotaging the car. He'd merely smiled and held up the distributor cap, then helped her out of the disabled Corvette.

"I'm going into town for a while this afternoon," he told her once she was again dressed in jeans and a T-shirt Moss had managed to pack for her before he'd kidnapped her.

Kat was trying to stay angry at him but not wholly succeeding at it. She wasn't only beginning to admire his incorrigibility more than she ought to; she was fairly certain she was starting to like it.

"Am I allowed to go along?" she asked, sitting on the couch, her shoes in her hand.

Moss pursed his lips, his gray eyes gleaming. "I don't think you're ready or willing to behave yourself in public yet, do you?"

Kat sighed. "I guess that means no." It also meant she was going to get another chance at escape, whether she wanted it or not.

"I'll stay here if you think you'll be too lonely," Moss offered, apparently determined to goad her.

"Don't change your plans on my account," Kat cooed. "I'm sure I'll survive without you." In truth, she wasn't at all sure she could. She wasn't even sure she wanted to anymore.

Something flickered in Moss's expression, but he said calmly, "In that case, give me your shoes."

Kat blinked up at him. "My what?"

"Your shoes. I can't leave you here by yourself without doing something to keep you here," he explained, "now can I? It's approximately ten miles to the nearest house," he told her as she handed over her loafers with a deadly look. "I wouldn't recommend trying to do it in bare feet. I'll be back in an hour or so. Try not to get into any trouble."

Damn the man, he was enjoying himself!

With a determined glitter in her eyes, Kat watched him drive back down the dusty expanse of road. She knew exactly what she was going to do as soon as the black Corvette was out of sight. She was going to try to escape. She felt obligated at least to make an attempt at it. Any self-respecting prisoner would, she reasoned.

She gave the road a cursory glance, then started moving. She wasn't afraid of walking. It would have been easier if Moss had left her her shoes, of course, but it still wasn't impossible to negotiate the stony surface . . .

. . . but it *was* close to impossible, she conceded half an hour later as she carefully picked her way over the sharp rocks jutting out of the hard-packed earth. She estimated she was only halfway down to the main road, and already she was tired and thirsty. Perspiration matted her hair against her forehead and neck. The slight breeze humming through the pines didn't even begin to cool her.

Pausing briefly, Kat sat down on a boulder beside the road to rest in the shade of a tall stand of ponderosa pines. Bending over, she plucked a thistle from her right foot. Surrounded by air redolent of pine and the dried-herb fragrance of summer-scorched grass, Kat leaned back against the rough bark of the closest tree and shut her eyes for a few seconds. She allowed herself only a brief respite. Then, shaking herself out of her growing lethargy, she started to get up . . . and immediately discovered she'd gotten pitch all over her back. A *lot* of pitch. A lot of sticky, sun-warmed pitch.

Wresting herself away from the tree, Kat stood up, surveyed the damage to her blue T-shirt and the dirt-laden condition of her bare feet, and let out a muffled oath of despair.

Damn Moss, she swore, cautiously returning to the road. He was the one who'd gotten her into this ridiculous situation in the first place. She was exhausted, and she didn't even know where she was going, for heaven's sake. And when she got there, wherever it was, she was going to arrive looking like a very disreputable refugee. She'd be lucky if they didn't call the police and put *her* in jail!

The main highway finally came into sight. Kat could hear the low buzz of a truck in the distance as it shifted gears.

"Well, hallelujah," she muttered.

She'd taken perhaps two more steps when, from behind her, Moss's voice rang out in the stillness of the forest.

"I was wondering how far you'd get," he drawled.

CHAPTER
Fifteen

EXPECT THE UNEXPECTED, Moss had once said. But Kat had never imagined he might be referring to himself.

Her eyes widened as he leaned away from the tree and surveyed her bedraggled condition without expression. "Were you going to leave without saying good-bye, then?" he asked. If she'd had hackles, she decided fleetingly, they'd be rising at a precipitous pace.

"Moss," she said, nervously licking her lips, "you just don't understand—"

"Make me understand. Make me understand why you're willing to give up so easily on us. Why you're so ready to trash our relationship."

Kat lifted her hands, then dropped them back down to her sides. "What kind of relationship do we have?"

"A good one, I thought," he said calmly.

"No." Kat shook her head slowly, sadly. "One based on false premises. Oh, Moss." She sighed in almost aching despair. "No matter what you say, no matter how many times you deny it, you love me because you still think I'm in need of protection."

"And you're not?"

"No," said Kat, wishing she could lie, "I'm not. Like it or not, I'm perfectably capable of looking out for myself."

"So prove it."

The velvety words had been so softly spoken, Kat wasn't sure she'd heard right. "What?"

"I said prove it," he repeated. This time Kat couldn't miss the underlying note of challenge. Feet spaced wide apart, hands fisted on his narrow hips, Moss had never looked taller or stronger or more dangerous. "Don't keep telling me how competent you are at taking care of yourself." He smiled, and that smile made Kat swallow convulsively. "Stick around and prove it."

Kat didn't want to prove it. She wanted to run in the other direction as fast as her feet would carry her. "If you're suggesting that I actually *fight* you—"

"That's exactly what I'm suggesting. If you're so good at taking care of yourself as you keep saying, it shouldn't be a problem."

If only that were true! "It's not going to work, Moss," she warned unsteadily. "I know what you're trying to do," she added, wishing she did.

"Do you?" he mused out loud. "I wonder."

"I'm not afraid of defending myself against anyone," Kat assured him, "including you."

But she was, and he knew it, even if he didn't fully comprehend the reason why. How could she explain? Defending herself against a real assailant was one thing. Fending off the man she loved, the man she wouldn't hurt for anything, was quite another matter. What if she somehow, despite the obvious disparities in their size, managed to deck him? The answer was easy. Like Derek, he would never, ever really forgive her. It would be the beginning of the end. She knew it as surely as she was standing there.

"If you're really not afraid to show me what you've got," he suggested softly, "then come here. Because I can guarantee you, accepting my challenge is the only way you're going to leave here."

Kat knew that anyone with even an ounce of good sense

would concede defeat and surrender at this point. Unfortunately, she had never been known for her good sense. Throwing caution to the wind, she inhaled and took a bold but not too big step toward him.

"Closer," Moss urged silkily. "I'm hard to convince." When she didn't move—couldn't, really, because that anticipatory gleam in his eye had suddenly rooted her to the spot—he shrugged. "Well, if Muhammad won't come to the mountain . . ."

He moved to within ten feet of her. Kat tensed in horrified expectation as she stared at the golden bronzed skin of his muscled arms, the breadth of his strong shoulders, the too-masculine build of his body beneath the black T-shirt and snug jeans.

Flailing around for at least a semblance of courage, Kat cast a disparaging eye over his attire, and then her own. "What's it going to be? Jeans at twenty paces?"

Moss calmly removed his ankle-high boots. "I was thinking more in the way of hand-to-hand combat." Before she knew what he was up to, he reached out for her. Split seconds later, Kat found herself sprawled on the soft cushion of pine needles covering the ground.

"What the devil do you think you're doing?" she squeaked, glaring up at his extended hand as he reached down and helped her back to her feet.

"I'm going to give you a crash course on how to surrender gracefully," he told her with utter calm. "I love your fire, Kat. Your persistence. Your determination. You've got more life in you than any woman I've ever known. But you haven't learned yet there are times when it's wise—no, imperative—to admit defeat." He paused, his gray eyes somber. "If I do nothing else, I'm going to teach you when to give up."

"I knew I should've told you to go to the devil the first time I met you," Kat said in a dubious attempt at humor.

"Too late now," said Moss with a show of white teeth. "Besides, if I recall correctly, you did."

Kat sighed. "I guess I did, much good it did me." She

gave him a hopeful smile. "How about us discussing this over a cup of coffee?"

"Can't," said Moss with a shake of his head. "I don't want to see you get hurt, and that's what's going to happen if you keep on the way you've been doing. Words don't seem to make much of an impression on you. Neither does experience, apparently. I thought you'd learned that night your apartment was broken into, but it was obvious the next morning that nothing had changed. You seem to have this idea you're indestructible." His smile was grim now. "No one's indestructible, Kat. Not even you."

Alarmed at the turn the situation had taken, Kat started to explain she didn't think any such thing, but Moss lifted a large hand to silence her. "I know what you're going to say. You're not trying to prove how brave you are, just that you're independent. What you don't seem to recognize is that there's a difference between being independent and being foolish. In your desire to prove what a competent private eye you are, the line of demarcation has apparently gotten fuzzy. I'm going to help clarify things for you a little."

Lord, he was serious, Kat realized a little wildly. He really intended to draw her into physical confrontation! He wanted to teach her a lesson. What if she ended up teaching him one, instead?

"I'm not going to hurt you," he assured her as she stared at him with disbelieving gray-green eyes. "I might hurt your pride a little, but I'd rather do that than see you crash around the way you've been doing."

Kat swallowed dryly. He wouldn't hurt her, he said. But what if she hurt him? Specifically, what if she hurt his pride? What then?

"Don't look at me like that," he scolded, beginning to move to his left. "There's nothing to be afraid of."

That's what you think! Kat thought, reluctantly countering by moving to her own left.

"Think of the worst thing that can happen," Moss suggested, obviously trying to reassure her she was safe from all but a few bruises.

"I am," said Kat, "I am." She'd thought of it endlessly, and the answer was always the same: She'd turn his love into hate, and that was why she'd tried to run away. It would be just like what had happened with Derek. She couldn't risk it. She *wouldn't* risk it. She'd rather let Moss think she was a dithering idiot than risk seeing his change in attitude if she managed to floor him.

Moss feinted to the right, and Kat jumped back and edged away.

"What are you afraid of?" he chided as she continued to try to put more distance between them. "I've already told you I won't hurt you."

"I know what you told me," Kat retorted. "I'm hard to convince."

Shaking his head, Moss stopped moving. "I never thought you were a coward," he said, plainly trying to goad her into action.

"But I am," Kat insisted. "I am a coward. A very big coward." Let him think she was terrified for all the wrong reasons, she decided. It was safer than the alternative!

"It's not your self-image you're worried about, is it?" he asked. And when Kat didn't answer, one tawny eyebrow rose. "Is it mine?" When Kat still didn't answer, he looked surprised, and then something else she couldn't quite identify. "It is, isn't it?" he said almost in wonder.

Hesitating, then giving in, Kat said tersely, "Yes!"

Plainly nonplussed, Moss stared at her for a long moment. Then his mouth curved. "Let me get this straight, once and for all. You're afraid to fight me not because you're afraid of getting hurt, but because you're afraid I'm going to get my ego battered?"

He sounded so incredulous, Kat felt a sharp stab of annoyance. "Don't think that just because you're big I couldn't give you a run for your money. Stranger things have happened!"

"Ah." He nodded in understanding. "You've got that look on your face again. Let me guess. You once battled Derek, right? What did he do, insist on a duel of the sexes?"

Kat eyed him stonily. "Not exactly."

"What exactly?"

"We were horsing around," Kat said, her voice tight. "And I accidentally threw him." She paused, then added, "Flat on his back."

"And?" Moss prompted.

"And he never forgave me."

"And you think that if you manage to throw me, history is going to repeat itself," Moss guessed. When Kat nodded grimly, he shrugged. "Well, we'll just have to see about that, won't we?"

Kat stared at him in genuine horror, remembering Derek's face when she had obeyed his laughing challenge and then laid him flat on his back with dismaying ease. And how their marriage had disintegrated soon after that.

"You still want me to fight you?" she asked in disbelief. "Even after what I told you?"

"I think it's more important than ever now." He tucked in his T-shirt. "Don't you? Otherwise, you're going to keep worrying about it. You've obviously been stewing about it from the very beginning." He smiled at her in mild exasperation. "I wish I'd guessed sooner just what it was that was keeping us apart. I'm not Derek, Kat. I've told you that before. Guess it's time to prove it." He beckoned her forward. "Come on, show me what you can do."

Lord, that was the last thing she wanted to do! "What you're saying," she said, staying put, "is that you're going to let me flip you so you can prove what a liberated man you are. No thanks."

"I don't mean anything of the sort." He took off his belt and threw it to one side. "What I'm saying is that I want you to try to down me. I want you to give it your best shot, too, because I'm going to mean business, I assure you."

Kat wasn't assured of anything. "Aren't you forgetting something?" she asked. "I know karate. In fact, I teach self-defense."

"I know you do." Moss sounded calm, even unconcerned. "For free. The guy at the Y said you refuse to take any money for it. But your knowing karate will just make this that much more interesting, don't you agree?"

"No." Kat shook her head, her loose russet hair swinging freely.

"No, you don't agree? Or no, you won't do it?"

"Both."

"Why? Because you're afraid after all this bragging you might not win anyway?"

He was deliberately goading her again. Kat simply gave him a cool stare. "I am *not*," she said with an adamant shake of her head, "going to fight—"

She never got to finish. Moss moved forward, and again she was yanked, lifted, and dropped to the ground. Kat curled her head under and rolled to minimize the shock. It still knocked the wind out of her.

"You okay?" Moss stood over her with a look of concern on his face.

Kat glared up at him, then allowed him to pull her to her feet. Gritting her teeth, she picked the pine needles from her hair.

"Maybe we'd better kick these pine cones out of the way," Moss suggested, bending over.

Resisting a strong urge to flip him onto his gluteus maximus with a swift leg lift, Kat helped him pick up the debris scattered over the small clearing. But as she did so, she couldn't help noticing the way Moss kept favoring his left side. Straightening, she looked at him in open suspicion.

"What's wrong with your left shoulder?" He hadn't been disguising the injury, whatever it was, she noted. Which proved what? That he was careless? Impossible. More likely, he didn't think it was going to matter because he didn't believe she was going to be much of a match for him.

"I hurt it when I fell off the cabin roof this morning, checking the chimney," he admitted. "Don't worry about it. I'm right-handed."

Don't worry about it? Kat rolled her eyes in disgust. How could she not worry about it? "You know, if Laurel and Candy-Anna are responsible for Mark's troubles, we ought to be apprehending them."

Moss smiled at her obvious attempt to halt the match. "That comes next. Right after we finish our business here."

The next time he lunged at her, all Kat could do was think about his injured shoulder. She didn't hesitate long— perhaps a second or two—but it was all Moss needed to take advantage of her. She started to block and parry, re- alized she was going to hit him where it hurt, started to withdraw . . . and ended up on her posterior.

"Ooof!"

Kat sat on the cushion of pine needles and wondered just how much physical punishment she could take. And how much of that self-satisfied smile on Moss's face she could put up with.

He stood over her, clucking his tongue. "Stop sandbag- ging," he scolded, dragging her back to her feet. "Or are you really this inept?"

Kat eyed him warily from a distance of about five feet. The arrogant beast! His methods, so far, were pretty ham- fisted but remarkably successful. He obviously knew a few maneuvers. The question was, how many and how well?

Kat chewed her lower lip, trying to decide what to do. Part of her was irritated. Moss looked like a man intent on bringing her to her knees. Literally. But part of her was excited. He was big—Lord, was he big! But being big wasn't always an advantage. His center of gravity was higher. Theoretically, that should make it easier to put him off- balance. But since he was so big, he also had a very long reach. She couldn't get too close to him. Her eyes fell to his strong wrists and hands, and she felt a tremor that had absolutely nothing to do with fear ripple through her. Trying to be dispassionate, she mentally categorized and listed all his strengths and his precious few weaknesses. His lean body was so exquisitely male, so perfectly built. But as strong as he was physically, Moss might still be fragile when it came to his ego. No matter what he said.

"Kat?"

The soft prompting brought her to attention. Slowly, almost imperceptibly, Moss was moving again to his left, circling her, putting her on his strong side. Kat knew he was going to try to fell her again. Still she didn't expect the quick movement when it came. She saw his leg swing out, jumped back, felt his hands latch on to her upper arms. Then came the unsettling sensation of losing her balance, being lifted, turned, and dropped down onto the needle-soft ground with a decisive *thump!*

Surprised and breathless, Kat stared up at Moss as he smiled benignly down at her. "Weren't you ready?"

The mocking question set her teeth on edge. Getting to her feet again, this time under her own steam, she brushed off her jeans and faced him more warily, studying the graceful way he moved, the fluid motions of his muscles. The intimate contact with his body, however brief, was doing terrible things to her composure...

She saw him coming this time. She still couldn't seem to do anything about it. He countered her reflexive move easily, as if he'd guessed what she was going to do. Which was impossible, Kat thought wildly as she felt herself losing her footing once again, unless he—

It hit her at the same time he gently but decisively pulled her to the ground.

"You know judo!" she accused, glaring up at him as he towered over her.

"Jujitsu," he corrected blandly.

Kat groaned and flopped back in despair. Karate, her speciality, essentially consisted of hand and foot blows; judo was basically throwing and grappling; and aikido was holds and locks. Jujitsu was a combination of all three, one of the most versatile of all the martial arts . . . and one of the hardest to deal with.

"I suppose you're pretty good at it, too," Kat ventured. Moss nodded and she asked hopefully, "Brown belt?" His tawny head moved side to side, and Kat let out a long, tired sigh. "Don't tell me. Black belt, right?"

"Up on your feet," Moss commanded with disgusting cheerfulness. "We're not through yet."

Somehow, Kat had known he was going to say that.

Slowly rising, she contemplated the man before her. She knew now, just as surely as she loved him, that she was going to have to fight him. His ego and her pride demanded it.

More carefully now, she considered his size, his quickness, his determination. The basic principle of self-defense was to use the least amount of force necessary to stop an intended assault. In her self-defense class for women, Kat emphasized avoidance, teaching behavior to minimize the possibility of assault. Helping other women learn how to avoid being a victim, learn how to be assertive yet neither passive nor aggressive, learn to be prepared to defend themselves but not overly eager to do so, was something she enjoyed teaching, and she did it very well.

None of that was going to help her now.

Not only was it going to be impossible to avoid fighting Moss, she wasn't sure she wanted to anymore. She didn't even want to use the least amount of force necessary. What she *really* wanted to do was flip him onto his backside and wipe that aggravating expression off his face. And then make passionate love to him on the forest floor.

With what she considered an Academy Award–winning performance, Kat allowed him to down her one more time. Then, smiling inwardly, she took his proffered hand to help her up, waited until he was slightly off-balance, and then . . .

It wasn't easy to get him off his feet, Kat decided as a stunned-looking Moss rolled harmlessly and skillfully to the ground. It took a lot of effort and the element of surprise to accomplish it, but that expression on his face was worth it. She hoped.

"You little she-devil!" he uttered in amazement as he got to his feet and once more faced her.

He didn't look angry, Kat reflected as she nervously waited for his reaction. He didn't look threatened. And his shoulder had certainly healed with surprising rapidity!

"You faker!" she accused. "You're not hurt at all!"

Moss smiled, unrepentant. "I lied. Actually," he amended, "it was a half lie. I did fall off the cabin roof, but it was over a month ago. The shoulder is well healed by now."

"Then why tell me it still hurt?" Kat asked, genuinely puzzled.

"Flip me again," he urged, "and I'll consider telling you."

Kat didn't want to flip him again. She figured once was

pushing things to the limit. But Moss seemed determined to force the issue. He feinted to the right, moved to the left, and Kat, reacting instinctively, kicked out, hooked him on the ankle, and watched in horror as he toppled over.

Lord, she hadn't meant to do that!

Moss rose to one knee and gave her a crooked smile. "I'm not sure who's learning more here, me or you. You're quick, aren't you?"

But not quick enough. This time Kat went down so fast she wasn't even sure how it happened. She retaliated just as swiftly.

Flat on his back, Moss looked up, surprise and admiration gleaming in his smoke-dark eyes.

"Feeling threatened yet?" Kat asked, only half jokingly.

"Not yet." Moss got to his feet. "I dare you to do that again."

Egged on, Kat straightened her T-shirt and tried—hard— to repeat the feat. Refusing to acknowledge defeat even though a sheen of perspiration had formed on both their faces, she spun and kicked, blocked and counterblocked, coming close to downing Moss again and again only to fail as he moved quickly out of her reach. But it wasn't just the exertion that was raising her temperature. Relentlessly, Moss teased and tantalized her, bringing his muscled body up against hers in lingering contact until hot silver licked through her veins.

Feint and parry, move and countermove, Kat tried to ignore the glow of desire stoking up inside her. But there was something astonishingly erotic about coming into physical contact with Moss, especially when on the surface it had nothing whatsoever to do with passion. Beneath the surface, however, the awareness sizzling between them was enough to cause a forest fire of impressive magnitude.

Finally, with a burst of energy, Moss ended the exchange. Charging unexpectedly, he hooked her around the waist with his right arm and took her to the ground with him, pinning her there with his body.

The air whooshed out of Kat's lungs. "Good grief," she panted. "Just how much do you weigh, anyhow?"

"Not enough to ever keep you in line, I'll bet. Are you ready to surrender?" he demanded. When Kat stalled, pretending to make up her mind, he smiled weakly and pleaded, "Please say yes. I don't think I can keep this up much longer."

He was sprawled atop her, his long, lean body touching hers from her waist down. Savoring the feel of him, the way his body fitted neatly with hers, Kat relaxed her muscles and felt the tension flow out of Moss.

"That's more like it." He was just starting to smile in victory when Kat, deciding he was at his most vulnerable, rolled over, putting him on the bottom.

"Now are you feeling threatened?" she asked sweetly, pinning his outstretched arms with her own.

"Why you sneaky little—" In the middle of the sentence, Moss rolled back onto her. "Now do you surrender?" he mimicked, his eyes dark with unhidden desire.

A surge of unadulterated love flowed through Kat as she smiled serenely up at him. "Do you?"

"I'm considering it," he growled, cupping a hand over her breast. His eyebrows abruptly shot upward. "Why aren't you wearing a bra?" he scolded, fondling her unconfined nipple with his thumb.

"Because you forgot to pack me any."

"Ah," Moss nodded solemnly, "so I did. I don't think I'm going to be able to keep my hands off you," he admitted, sliding his hand up beneath her damp T-shirt, "now that I know you're half-naked."

"So what else is new?" Kat replied pertly.

Moss's warm, rough hand caressed her skin, his fingers tracing lazy circles around her breasts. "I suppose it's too much to hope you don't have any panties on."

"That's for me to know," Kat responded with a flirty smile, "and you to find out."

With a husky groan, Moss covered her lips with his, pouring out his desire in a flood of fierce kisses that left her breathless but desiring more. As if in answer, his tongue slipped between her teeth, demanding her response. Her pulse fluttering like a butterfly, Kat lay still beneath him,

absorbing the heat of him, returning his kisses until she was
sure they would both melt, consumed in the caldron of their
love.

His mouth locked onto hers, Moss pulled her up until
they were both on their knees, facing each other. "Undress
me," he murmured against her mouth, blazing a trail of hot,
teasing kisses across her lower lip, across her chin, down
her throat, and back again.

"Someone will come," Kat whispered on a quick intake
of breath as his fingers found the zipper on her jeans, taking
it down slowly, slowly . . .

"Let them," Moss murmured, slipping the denim down
over her slender hips, sliding his hands inside her panties
and removing them, too, even more slowly, as if prolonging
the pleasure of seeing her silky skin exposed in the filtered
forest light.

Her knees rapidly turning to Jello-O, Kat unbuttoned his
Levi's and pushed them down, her hands gliding over his
coarser limbs. Groaning, Moss pulled her even closer.

The physical evidence of his mounting desire filled Kat
with a sudden, deep, unexpectedly primitive desire to be
dominated. Eased onto the soft carpet of pine needles, she
traced the powerful ridges of muscle and bone in his back,
running her fingers down the length of his lean body to
the part of him that wasn't darkly tanned. She reveled in
the strength of him, savored the maleness of him, basked
in the restrained power of the hard, rippling muscles of his
thighs as his right knee nudged her legs apart.

"Kat," he murmured softly. "My sweet Kat."

His body slid smoothly over hers, joining them at last,
his hands strong and steady. Kat clung to him as their passion
rose slowly, steadily, inevitably, flaring and finally bursting
into a kaleidoscope of brightly colored glass, shattering into
fragments drifting like ashes on the soft, pine-scented air.

Kat lay in his arms, contented, knowing she'd never
again have to worry about threatening his masculinity. It
was intact, strong and as unshakable as ever. The battle was
over, and each was the victor.

"God, I love you." Moss's molten eyes raked her kiss-softened mouth, and a new tide of silver warmth flowed through her. "Tell me you love me."

"I love you," Kat whispered, her passion-flushed face evidence of the truth of her words. "I love you, I love you, I love you."

"One more time," Moss smiled tenderly. "I'm a hard man to convince."

"I love you," Kat returned obediently. "More than life itself."

"Oh, Kat." Moss groaned and buried his face in her neck, nuzzling the exquisitely sensitive spot behind her ear. "I don't think I'm ever going to get tired of hearing you say that."

"That's good." Kat wrinkled her nose. "Because you're going to be hearing it a lot."

"Promises, promises." Shifting to one side, he dropped kisses all the way from her mouth to her navel and back again.

The sharp scent of pine filled Kat's senses. Whenever she smelled it in the future, she knew she would always remember this moment.

"We should probably get dressed," she murmured reluctantly as Moss turned his attention to the area around her hipbone and began a trek downward. "Someone might come."

"Don't worry," said Moss, "we've already got an audience."

"We *what?*"

Kat started to bolt upright, but Moss deftly pushed her down and rolled back on top of her. "There's no need to shout," he said mildly.

"Who . . . where . . . ?"

"My friend Satchmo," said Moss, "over there behind you."

Steeling herself, Kat tipped her head back and discovered a ground squirrel, cheeks stuffed with booty, watching them with bright black eyes filled with curiosity.

"He's probably wondering what the devil we're doing,"

Moss mused as Kat sighed in relief.

"Don't tell him," she said firmly. "He's probably underage."

"Let's give him a show he'll never forget," Moss suggested, leveling his body over hers once again.

It wasn't until Kat saw her left hand that she realized the dampness she felt on Moss's back wasn't wholly perspiration. It was blood.

"You've hurt yourself!" she gasped. "Did I . . . when we . . ."

"No! Get that look off your face." Moss kissed her hard on the mouth. "I did that when I fell off the roof this morning. Stop worrying. It's nothing."

"But you said that was a month ago!"

His mouth twisted wryly. "I lied. I didn't want you to hold back because you thought I was hurt. It's really not bad," he added in dubious reassurance. "Just a cut."

Kat groaned in exasperation. "And here I was beginning to think you weren't the macho type. You take terrible care of yourself," she admonished sternly, panting slightly from their recent physical exertion and Moss's considerable weight pinning her to the forest floor. "You're worse than a child."

"You should talk." Moss ran a gruffly caressing hand over her tumbled red hair. "You've got all the self-preservation instincts of a flea." His fingers moved with aching slowness across her cheek to her throat. "You need looking after."

"*I* never fell off a roof in my life," Kat assured him, increasingly aware of the pressure of his hips, the way they perfectly fitted to her own. "You worry about everyone's welfare but your own. Don't you think it's high time you did something about it? If you're not going to take care of yourself," she continued breathlessly, wondering whatever had happened to her pride, "you ought to have somebody around who will."

Moss smiled then, and his mouth descended the last remaining inch toward hers. "For once we agree," he murmured, sealing her lips with his own. "I was thinking exactly the same thing."

CHAPTER
Sixteen

THE STUDIO WAS darkened, with only the soft glow of a chandelier for illumination. Ten background models, dressed in silks, jewels, and furs, milled around the room while Mark Adams stood by his camera, readying it for the photo session about to take place. Kat and Moss stood in the concealing shadows of myriad props, waiting to spring the trap they'd set.

"Are you sure it's them?" Kat asked, stretching her shoulder muscles, which were still sore from her bout with Moss.

Moss automatically reached up and gently kneaded the tendons at the nape of her neck. "Absolutely positive. You think there still might be a chance it's someone else?"

"Well, we don't actually have any proof yet other than Emma Li's testimony, and frankly I don't trust people who testify in exchange for immunity. Besides that, Laurel and Candy-Anna were both sabotaged themselves right in front of me."

The fingers on her neck moved down her spine. "Haven't you been wondering about the timing of those two incidents?"

"What do you mean?"

"They both happened on the same day, within minutes of each other. Tell me something. Did you do anything earlier that day that might have made either woman nervous?"

Kat felt her muscles relax beneath his touch. "Well, I asked Laurel a few questions about what was going on. You don't think—?"

"Yes, as a matter of fact, I do. She probably realized it was time both she and Candy-Anna joined the ranks of the sabotaged models before you started asking any more embarrassing questions."

"Candy-Anna could've started the fire in the darkroom," Kat admitted after a moment. "She definitely had the opportunity. But I can't believe she set herself up with the snake. Believe me, she wasn't acting that time. She was scared out of her wits."

"That's because she knew Laurel had set up some sort of booby-trap earlier that morning, but she didn't know exactly what. And because she's got a phobia about reptiles. That's why Laurel planted the snake. She knew Candy-Anna's reaction to it would remove her from suspicion, just like the burned film would deflect attention away from herself. She had to do something quick, before you got too nosy. Still not convinced? Then think about that list you made up, and you'll realize that every time something was stolen either Laurel or Candy-Anna or Emma Li was there. But, more important, Laurel was always in the studio sometime *before* all hell broke loose."

"The beach props," Kat suddenly remembered. "Laurel had been in again that afternoon, saying she'd left something behind."

"Another thing. Had you noticed that almost every time a model refused to return, Mark invariably hired Laurel in her place? That's because she volunteered to fill in when the secretaries left, making sure she was always around and available. She couldn't lose."

Kat grimaced. "Multiple motives and multiple culprits. No wonder it took you so long to make sense of it."

"I probably never would have if it hadn't been for you. They must have thought they had it made until you showed up. All the other secretaries were easy to scare off. Which reminds me—did you realize the reason the secretaries left with such regularity was because Laurel always informed them of the dire facts of their predecessors just prior to pulling a string of nasties on them?"

"I'd wondered," Kat admitted. "Can I ask you another question? Why didn't you catch Laurel or Candy-Anna with the hidden camera?"

"Because Laurel always placed the changing screens in the way, and Mark objected to my putting another camera in the models' dressing area. Laurel is apparently the ring-leader, according to Emma Li. And the one, I'd be willing to bet, who broke into your apartment that night."

Kat leaned against him and shook her head. "Our 'be-jeweled, jet-setting partygoers' look properly elegant, but I still can't believe Yan Bagdasarian in that ruffled shirt and cummerbund."

"You'd think Yan had always hankered to be a male model, the way he's taking to the part," Moss agreed. "But it seems inconceivable that with all this junk around we had to borrow a velvet tuxedo jacket from your brother." He paused. "It was nice of Ken to cooperate."

"Nice nothing." Kat sniffed. "He's hoping it'll keep me from locking him out of my fridge for the rest of our natural lives. Speaking of brothers, Mark's certainly taking this setup calmly. Especially since we're hoping to snare two of his favorite models."

"It was his idea to use the special camera and infrared film. I think he's looking forward to catching them in the act."

Kat sighed. "I hope this works. If it doesn't, we're going to have a hard time coming up with enough hard evidence to nail them."

"Once Mark gets them on film swiping the rubies, it's all the evidence we'll need. What's the matter? Nervous?"

"Me? No. I love the idea of being caught in the dark with you."

"Shameless woman. What am I going to do with you?"

"You need suggestions?"

"I dare you to say that when we're through here." Standing behind her, Moss ran his tongue over her ear, down her neck.

"If we ever get done here," said Kat, hot silver sliding warmly through her veins, "I'd be happy to. How's that bruise on your ankle?"

"Healing. I should've known better than to challenge a woman who wears a Miss Piggy watch. What time have you got?"

"Twenty past six. Lord, what if they don't show?"

"They'll show. Morgan made sure he told them the shoot would involve some very valuable jewelry, and Laurel thinks she booby-trapped the chandelier. They're just late. Like most women."

"Stop now, or you'll have a matching bruise on your other ankle."

Moss started to answer, then said, "Ah, I think I hear a car door outside. Ready?"

"Oh, no."

"What's the matter?"

"This blasted moosehead. I think I'm going to sneeze."

Spinning her around, Moss kissed her hard on the mouth. Stunned when he let go, Kat blinked up at him, the urge to sneeze abated. "A new remedy for stopping sneezes? Does it work with hiccups, too?"

Moss chucked her under the chin. "Pay attention, sweetheart. I think we're about to catch us some thieves."

In the end, it was almost disappointingly easy. Laurel Tandy and Candy-Anna Carpenter entered the studio within five minutes of each other. Both took quick but unsuspecting looks at Yan Bagdasarian, noted the tray of "extra" jewelry set to one side, and disappeared behind the dressing screens. Ten minutes later they reappeared and took their places before the camera along with the three policewomen Yan Bagdasarian had recruited to pose as models with him.

Mark had taken over twenty shots in various poses before Moss let the chandelier flicker the first time. Seven poses later, he let it flicker again. Five shots later he let it go out completely, immersing the studio in total blackness.

On cue, the policewomen started complaining loudly, providing Laurel and Candy-Anna with enough covering noise for them to steal a chattering monkey if they wanted to. Moss gave them a good half minute, just to be sure, then flooded the studio with light. For a moment both women stood blinking in surprise at Kat and Moss emerging from behind the tangle of props, but it wasn't until the policewomen clamped handcuffs over the models' wrists and began reciting them their rights that they seemed to realize what had happened.

"What do you think you're doing?" Laurel began before glancing down. Instead of disappearing into the folds of their evening gowns, the stolen rubies had attached themselves to both her and Candy-Anna's hands. The faceted red stones winked in the bright light.

"Caught red-handed, as it were," Moss murmured as the two stunned women were led away, with Mark following to file charges.

"Definitely two culprits with sticky fingers," Kat agreed, adding, "I do hope that glue comes off. Manny Manetti didn't mind lending us the rubies, but I think he expects them back."

"Considering how much we had to pay him for renting them, we ought to be able to keep them at least a year. But if he starts to get nasty about it, I'll let you deal with him. The man scares me to death." After safely retrieving the remaining jewels from the departing extras, Moss locked the studio and held out his arm. "Coming, Mrs. Adams? I believe we still have the small matter of our honeymoon to attend to."

Kat slipped her arm through his and let him lead her outside into the cool night air. She'd just started to shiver, whether from the cold or as a reaction to the last hour she wasn't sure, when she felt him pull her to him. He kissed her deeply and with love, his hands gently sweeping over her ribs to caress her breasts. "The wonders of quickie Nevada marriages," he chuckled softly against her hair. "We got rid of Langley's name and created a new partnership, all in one smooth move. How does Adams and Adams Investigative Agency sound?"

Kat leaned away and smiled up at him. "It sounds wonderful. Just don't get *too* complacent." She brushed her fingertips lightly over his chin. "Because this partner expects to share all things equally."

Moss smiled. "Not to worry, sweetheart. Complacent is the last thing I'll ever be around you. I may learn slow, but when I learn, I learn good." Again he slipped his arm through hers. "Come, love. We have a lifetime to spend together, starting now. And I don't want to waste a minute of it."

Second Chance at Love ®

___ 0-425-07773-X	INTRUDER'S KISS #246 Carole Buck	$2.25
___ 0-425-07774-8	LADY BE GOOD #247 Elissa Curry	$2.25
___ 0-425-07775-6	A CLASH OF WILLS #248 Lauren Fox	$2.25
___ 0-425-07776-4	SWEPT AWAY #249 Jacqueline Topaz	$2.25
___ 0-425-07975-9	PAGAN HEART #250 Francine Rivers	$2.25
___ 0-425-07976-7	WORDS OF ENDEARMENT #251 Helen Carter	$2.25
___ 0-425-07977-5	BRIEF ENCOUNTER #252 Aimée Duvall	$2.25
___ 0-425-07978-3	FOREVER EDEN #253 Christa Merlin	$2.25
___ 0-425-07979-1	STARDUST MELODY #254 Mary Haskell	$2.25
___ 0-425-07980-5	HEAVEN TO KISS #255 Charlotte Hines	$2.25
___ 0-425-08014-5	AIN'T MISBEHAVING #256 Jeanne Grant	$2.25
___ 0-425-08015-3	PROMISE ME RAINBOWS #257 Joan Lancaster	$2.25
___ 0-425-08016-1	RITES OF PASSION #258 Jacqueline Topaz	$2.25
___ 0-425-08017-X	ONE IN A MILLION #259 Lee Williams	$2.25
___ 0-425-08018-8	HEART OF GOLD #260 Liz Grady	$2.25
___ 0-425-08019-6	AT LONG LAST LOVE #261 Carole Buck	$2.25
___ 0-425-08150-8	EYE OF THE BEHOLDER #262 Kay Robbins	$2.25
___ 0-425-08151-6	GENTLEMAN AT HEART #263 Elissa Curry	$2.25
___ 0-425-08152-4	BY LOVE POSSESSED #264 Linda Barlow	$2.25
___ 0-425-08153-2	WILDFIRE #265 Kelly Adams	$2.25
___ 0-425-08154-0	PASSION'S DANCE #266 Lauren Fox	$2.25
___ 0-425-08155-9	VENETIAN SUNRISE #267 Kate Nevins	$2.25
___ 0-425-08199-0	THE STEELE TRAP #268 Betsy Osborne	$2.25
___ 0-425-08200-8	LOVE PLAY #269 Carole Buck	$2.25
___ 0-425-08201-6	CAN'T SAY NO #270 Jeanne Grant	$2.25
___ 0-425-08202-4	A LITTLE NIGHT MUSIC #271 Lee Williams	$2.25
___ 0-425-08203-2	A BIT OF DARING #272 Mary Haskell	$2.25
___ 0-425-08204-0	THIEF OF HEARTS #273 Jan Mathews	$2.25
___ 0-425-08284-9	MASTER TOUCH #274 Jasmine Craig	$2.25
___ 0-425-08285-7	NIGHT OF A THOUSAND STARS #275 Petra Diamond	$2.25
___ 0-425-08286-5	UNDERCOVER KISSES #276 Laine Allen	$2.25
___ 0-425-08287-3	MAN TROUBLE #277 Elizabeth Henry	$2.25
___ 0-425-08288-1	SUDDENLY THAT SUMMER #278 Jennifer Rose	$2.25
___ 0-425-08289-X	SWEET ENCHANTMENT #279 Diana Mars	$2.25

Prices may be slightly higher in Canada.

COMING NEXT MONTH
IN THE
SECOND CHANCE AT LOVE SERIES

QUESTIONNAIRE

1. How do you rate _____

   (please print TITLE)

   ☐ excellent   ☐ good
   ☐ very good   ☐ fair   ☐ poor

2. How likely are you to purchase another book
   in this series?
   ☐ definitely would purchase
   ☐ probably would purchase
   ☐ probably would not purchase
   ☐ definitely would not purchase

3. How likely are you to purchase another book by
   this author?
   ☐ definitely would purchase
   ☐ probably would purchase
   ☐ probably would not purchase
   ☐ definitely would not purchase

4. How does this book compare to books in other
   contemporary romance lines?
   ☐ much better
   ☐ better
   ☐ about the same
   ☐ not as good
   ☐ definitely not as good

5. Why did you buy this book? (Check as many as apply)
   ☐ I have read other
      SECOND CHANCE AT LOVE romances
   ☐ friend's recommendation
   ☐ bookseller's recommendation
   ☐ art on the front cover
   ☐ description of the plot on the back cover
   ☐ book review I read
   ☐ other _____
      _____
      _____

(Continued...)

6. Please list your three favorite contemporary romance lines.
_____
_____

7. Please list your favorite authors of contemporary romance lines.
_____
_____
_____
_____
_____
_____

8. How many SECOND CHANCE AT LOVE romances have you read? _____

9. How many series romances like SECOND CHANCE AT LOVE do you <u>read</u> each month? _____

10. How many series romances like SECOND CHANCE AT LOVE do you <u>buy</u> each month? _____

11. Mind telling your age?
    ☐ under 18
    ☐ 18 to 30
    ☐ 31 to 45
    ☐ over 45

☐ Please check if you'd like to receive our <u>free</u> SECOND CHANCE AT LOVE Newsletter.

We hope you'll share your other ideas about romances with us on an additional sheet and attach it securely to this questionnaire.

• •

Fill in your name and address below:
Name _____
Street Address _____
City _____ State _____ Zip _____

Please return this questionnaire to:
    SECOND CHANCE AT LOVE
    The Berkley Publishing Group
    200 Madison Avenue, New York, New York 10016